George Wright

The Gentleman's Miscellany

Consisting of Essays, Characters, Narratives, Anecdotes, and Poems...

T

Gentleman's Miſcellany

CONSISTING OF

ESSAYS, CHARACTERS, NARRATIVES;
ANECDOTES, and POEMS

MORAL AND ENTERTAINING

CALCULATED FOR

THE IMPROVEMENT OF GENTLEMEN IN
EVERY RELATION IN LIFE.

—o◠o—

By GEORGE WRIGHT, Esq.

EITOR OF THE LADY'S MISCELLANY, PLEASING
MELANCHOLY, RURAL CHRISTIAN, &c.

—o◠o—

Omne tulit punctum qui miſcuit utile dulci. Hor.

—o◠o—

𝔍iꞧſꞇ 𝔄merican 𝔈ꝺition.

Exeter.

PRINTED BY H. RANLET for WILLIAM T. CLAP, B
SOLD BY HIM, THOMAS & ANDREWS, E. LARKIN,
D. WEST, J. WITE, WM. P. L.
BLAKE, and C. B. JAM.
1797.

PREFACE.

————o⌇o————

THERE are few if any *material* points re-
specting the manners, conduct, and converfation of
Gentleman, but what .re infifted on and illuftrated i
the following pages. To admit the greater variety
of fubjects, fome lefs important, are only flightly
touched upon, while others more interefting, are
confidered and explained at large.

The duties of every relation in life, and the benefits refulting from the uniform practice of thofe duties, are held out and enforced both from examples
and experience. To enliven the moral and ferious
parts of this work, pleafing *Narratives*, *Anecdotes*, and
Poems, are interfperfed, which are intended to render it, agreeable to the *utile dulci* of the ancients,
both PROFITABLE and ENTERTAINING. How far it
is calculated to anfwer thefe purpofes, muft be left to
the decifion of the judicious and difcerning reader.

If any apology is thought neceffary for publifhing
this Mifcellany, it may be made in the remarks of
the

the Monthly Reviewers on a late similar publica-
tion of the Editor's, entitled, *Pleasing Reflections on
Life and Manners.*

" Miscellaneous collections of this kind are become
very numerous ; but as they generally consist of
moral pieces, they are, to say the least of them, innocent, as well as entertaining. The multiplicat on,
therefore, of such compilements, is of no diff
to society."

See MONTHLY REVIEW for AUG. 17

John-Street,   G. W.
April 23 1795.

CONTENTS.

CONTENTS.

A   *Contemplations*

vi CONTENTS.

Rational

Page

Rural

THE

THE

Gentleman's Mifcellany,

IN

PROSE AND VERSE.

————o᾽᷍ᴏ————

ON THE
DIFFERENT MANNERS OF READING;
OR,
DIRECTIONS FOR READING TO ADVANTAGE.

WHAT is any book, if it is not read in
that manner by which it may beft be underftood? A
novel, whofe merit lies chiefly in the ftory, fhould be
quickly paffed through * ; for the clofer you can
bring the feveral circumftances together, the better
If its merit confifts in character and fentiment, it
fhould be read much flower ; for the leaft obvious
parts of a character are frequently the moft beautiful;
and the propriety of a fentiment may eafily efcape
in a hafty perufal.

Detached thoughts ought to be dwelt on longer
than any other manner of writing ; for different fubjects following clofe, do rather confound than inftruct;
but if we allow ourfelves time to reflect, we may un-
derftand the author, and perhaps improve ourfelves.
Each thought fhould be confidered as a text, upon
which we ought to make a commentary.

Bayle's

————————

* Few *modern* novels are worth reading.

Bayle's manner of writing by text and note is generally decried, but without reason. When there is a necessity of proving the assertion by quotation, which was his case, no other way can be taken equally perspicuous. The authorites must be produced somewhere—they cannot be in the text, and if they are put at the end of the book, which is the modern fashion, how much more troublesome are they for referring to, than by being at the bottom of the page? The truth is, this is another instance of ignorance in the method of reading. Bayle, Harris, and other writers of this class, should have the text read first, which is quickly dispatch'd; then, begin again and take in the notes. By these means you preserve a connexion, and judge of the proofs of what is asserted.

None judge less favourably of an author than his intimate friends—their personal knowledge of him as a man, destroys a hundred delusions to his advantage as an author.—"Who is a hero to his valet-de-chambre?" said the great Condé; and he might have added, "or to his *friends?*" Besides the obvious reason for this, it is most likely that an author has, in his common conversation, made his friends acquainted with his sentiments long before they are communicated to the public. The consequence is, that to *them* his work is not new; and it is possible that they may take to themselves part of his merit; for I have known many instances, where a person has been told something by way of information, which he himself told to the informer.

An author's intimate acquaintance frequently do him more harm than avowed enemies. They show so many apprehensions on his account—they so much dread the censure he may incur, and the enemies he may create by his new opinions, &c.

All this betrays a want of confidence, and is very
                                                naturally

naturally fet down to their knowing fomething of the author and his works the world is not acquainted with.

It is certain, that the lefs *perfonal* knowledge we have of an author, the greater is our efteem for his productions ; of courfe, we commend thofe the moft, of whom we know the *leaft.*

THE
BENEFITS of READING and REFLECTION
IN
YOUNGER LIFE.

WHATEVER temporary relief diffipation may afford to the vigour of youth, and ardour of manhood, it will not give the fame pleafure to advanced age. Mental obfervations will then rife in delight as juvenile fpirits fubfide; and reading and reflection will then afford that confolation which gay amufements cannot give. Therefore to neglect the cultivation of the mind in juvenile years, has in fome fort the fame effect as neglecting to feed the body : A languor muft enfue in both, which leads to a fatal tendency ; befides, we ought to confider, that if we refufe to exert our faculties in the degree they are given at a vigorous time of life, our talents may be taken from us, at a feafon when we fhall moft want them, and have the moft poignant fenfe of their deprivation.

It is every perfon's duty to keep the mind as eafy as poffible in every ftate ; elfe why do we gratify the child in a change of toys, when its innocent fimplicity is only capable of finding beauty in a ftraw, or mufic in a key ? But thefe trifles cannot amufe us beyond our infant ftate : The boy is difgufted with them, and the man calls for ftill nobler recreations. Robuft exercife fuccceds ; but that will not do for

weak

weak hands and feeble knees, which accompany the
laft ftage of life. Then the produce of learning and
reading is an amazing confolation ! But the feeds
muft be fown in youth, otherwife the fruits cannot
be gathered in age. And what fruits can be gathered from a trifling kind of reading, which leaves nothing for the mind to feed on ? Life is far too fhort
and precious to be wafted in mere amufement, which
does but in a manner pamper us for a facrifice, by
deftroying the feeds of fortitude and virtue.

A well-educated mind will often afford a fumptu-
ous treat to its happy poffeffor, even in folitude ;
which gives opportunity for a more copious range
of thought, on fubjects which ennoble human nature.

Jemmy Saunter, and his fair fpoufe, abounded in
worldly wealth ; but, I muft not go further. Yes I
may, for their houfe was nobly furnifhed, and I was
obligingly fhown all their plate, trinkets, and expen-
five attire. I exhaufted all the fine things I was a-
ble to fay, in its praife. But this being the only
theme for converfation, as the novelty fubfided, the
joy was loft with me ; and finding myfelf incapable
of inverting more panegyric to offer at this fhrine of
vanity, I endeavoured to divert myfelf with a little
girl, and to fathom the depth of her capacity. But
the moft I could get her to fay was, *My mamma is a
lady of fortune*, which fhe had made a little fong of ;
and it was fo often reverberated in my ear, that I wifhed, for the fake of the mother, as well as the daugh-
ter, that her fortune had lain more in her *mind**.

THE

---

* The mind with ufeful knowledge ftor'd,
  Delight and pleafure will afford.

THE
BANKRUPT TRADESMAN,
WITHOUT
LOSS OR MISFORTUNE.

Beware of Extravagance.

A YOUNG man of good character, sets up in business with a moderate capital, and a good deal of
credit; and soon after marries a young woman,
with whom he gets a little ready money, and good
expectations on the death of a father, mother, uncle,
or aunt. In two or three years he finds that his business increases; but his own health, or his wife's, or
his child's, makes it necessary for him to take lodgings in the country. Lodgings are soon found to be
inconvenient, and for a very small additional expense
he might have a snug little box of his own. A snug
little box is taken, repaired, new-modelled, and fur-
nished.

Here he always spends his Sundays, and commonly carries a friend or two with him just to eat a bit
of mutton, and to see how comfortably he is situated
in the country. Visitors of this sort are not wanting. One is invited because he is a customer, another because he may assist him in his business, a third
because he is a relation of his own or his wife's, a
fourth because he is an old acquaintance, and a fifth
because he is very entertaining; besides many who
look in accidentally, and are prevailed on to stay to
dinner, although they have an engagement somewhere
else.

He now keeps his horses for the sake of exercise;
but as this is a solitary kind of pleasure which his
wife cannot share, and as the expence of a whisky
can be but trifling where a horse is already kept, a
whiskey is purchased, in which he takes out his wife

B   and

and his child as often as his time will permit.   After
all, driving a whiskey is but indifferent amusement
to sober people ; his wife too is timorous, and ever
since she heard of Mrs. Threadneedle's accident, by
the stumbling of her horse, will not set her foot in
one ; Besides the expence of a horse and whiskey,
with what is occasionally spent in coach-hire, falls so
little short of what his friend Mr. Harness asks for a
job-coach, that it would be ridiculous not to accept
of an offer that never may be made him again.

'The job-coach is agreed for, and the boy in a plain
coat with a red cape to it, that used to clean the
knives, wait at table, and look after the horse, becomes a smart footman with a handsome livery. The
snug little box is now too small for so large a family.
There is a charming house, with a garden, and two
or three acres of land, rather farther from London,
but delightfully situated, the unexpired lease of which
might be had a great bargain. "The premises, to be
sure, are somewhat more extensive than he should
want, but the house is new, and, for a moderate expense, might be put into most excellent repair.

Hither he removes ; hires a gardener, being fond
of botany, and supplies his own table with every thing
in season, for little more than double the money the
same articles would cost if he went to market for
them.   Every thing about him now seems comfortable ; but his friend Harness does not treat him so
well as he expected.   His horses are often ill match-
ed, and the coachman sometimes even peremptorily
refuses to drive them a few miles extraordinary, for
why, " he's answerable to Master for the poor beasts."
His expenses, it is true, are as much as he can afford;
but having coach-house and stables of his own, with
two or three acres of excellent grass, he might certainly keep his own coach and horses for less money
than he pays to. Harness. A rich relation of his

wife's

wife's too is dying, and has often promifed to leave her fomething handfome.

The job-coach is difcharged, he keeps his own carriage, and his wife is now able to pay and receive many more vifits than fhe could before. Yet he finds by experience, that an airing in a carriage is but a bad fubftitute for a ride on horfeback, in the way of exercife ; he muft have a faddle-horfe ; and fubfcribes to a neighbouring hunt for his own fake, and to the neareft affemblies for the fake of his wife.

During all this progrefs, his bufinefs has not been neglected ; but his capital, originally fmall, has never been augmented. His wife's rich relations die one after another, and remember her only by trifling legacies ; his expenfes are evidently greater than his income ; and in a very few years, with the beft intentions in the world, and wanting no good quality but forefight to avoid, or refolution to retrench expences which his bufinefs cannot fupport ; his country-houfe and equipage, affifted by the many good friends who almoft conftantly dine with him, drive him fairly into the Gazette.

The country-houfe is let, the equipage is fold, his friends fhrug up their fhoulders, inquire for how much he has failed, wonder it was not for more, fay he was a good creature and an honeft creature ; but they always thought it would come to this, pity him from their very fouls, hope his creditors will be favourable to him, and go to find dinners elfewhere.

———o⌒o———

REFLECTIONS

ON

SYMPATHY AND COMPASSION.

———

Weep with thofe that weep.

THE word Sympathy, in its moft proper and primitive fignification, denotes our fellow-feeling with the fufferings of others. It is, in fome fenfe, more univerfal than that of joy. What we feel does not, indeed, amount to that complete fympathy, to that harmony and correfpondence of fentiments, which conftitute approbation. We do not weep, exclaim, and lament, with the fufferer. We are fenfible, on the contrary, of his weaknefs, and of the extravagance of his paffion, and yet often feel a very fenfible concern on his account. But if we do not entirely enter into, and go along with, the joy of another, we have no fort of regard or fellow-feeling for it. The man who fkips and dances about with that intemperate and thoughtlefs joy which we cannot accompany him in, is the object of our contempt and indignation.

Our fympathy with pain, though it falls greatly fhort of what is naturally felt by the fufferer, is generally a more lively and diftinct perception than our fympathy with pleafure. Certain it is, we often ftruggle hard to keep down our fympathy with the forrows of others. For, whenever we are not under the obfervation of the fufferer, we endeavour for our own fake, to fupprefs it as much as we can, and yet are not always fuccefsful. But we never have occafion to make this oppofition to our fympathy with joy. We often feel a fympathy with forrow, when we would wifh to be rid of it; and we often mifs that with joy when we would be glad to have it. The man, who, under the greateft calamities, can command his forrow, feems worthy of the higheft admiration; but he, who, in the fulnefs of profperity, can in the fame manner mafter his joy, feems hardly to deferve any praife.

What can be added to the happinefs of the man who is in health, out of debt, and has a clear confcience? To one in this fituation, all acceffions of fortune may properly be faid to be fuperfluous: But,

though

though little can be added to this state, much may be taken from it. Though between this condition and the higheſt pitch of human profperity, the interval is but a trifle ; between it and the loweſt depth of mifery, the diſtance is immenſe and prodigious. Adverfity, upon this account, neceſſarily depreſſes the mind of the ſufferer much more below its natural ſtate, than profperity can elevate him above it. It is, therefore, upon this account, that, however our ſympathy with ſorrow is often a more pungent ſenſation than our ſympathy with joy, it always falls very ſhort of the violence of what is naturally felt by the perſon principally concerned.

When we attend to the reprefentation of a tragedy, we ſtruggle againſt that ſympathetic ſorrow which the entertainment infpires as long as we can, and we give way to it at laſt only when we can no longer avoid it ; if we ſhed tears, we endeavour to conceal them, and are afraid leſt the ſpectators, not entering into this exceſſive tenderneſs, ſhould regard it as effeminacy and weakneſs. The wretch, whoſe misfortunes call upon our compaſſion, feels with what reluctance we are likely to enter into this ſorrow, and therefore propoſes his grief to us with fear and heſitation ; he even ſmothers the half of it, and is aſhamed, upon account of this hard-heartedneſs of mankind, to give vent to the fulneſs of his affliction. It is otherwiſe with the man who riots in joy and ſucceſs. Wherever envy does not intereſt us againſt him, he expects our completeſt ſympathy. He does not fear, therefore, to announce himſelf with ſhouts of exultation, in full confidence that we are heartily difpoſed to go along with him.

How hearty are the acclamations of the mob who never bear any envy to their ſuperiors at a triumph or public entry ? And how ſedate and moderate is commonly their grief at an execution ? Our ſorrow

at

at a funeral generally amounts to no more than an affected gravity; but our mirth at a chriftening, or a marriage, is always from the heart, and without any affectation.   On the contrary, when we condole with our friends in their afflictions, how little do we feel, in comparifon of what they feel? We fit down by them, we look at them, and, while they relate to us the circumftances of their misfortunes, we liften, it may be, to them with gravity and attention: But while their narration is every moment interrupted by thofe natural burfts of forrow, which often feem almoft to choak them in the midft of it, how far are the languid emotions of our hearts from keeping time to the pungent feelings of theirs? We may even inwardly reproach ourfelves with our own want of fenfibility, and perhaps, upon that account, work ourfelves up into an artificial fympathy; which, however, when it is raifed, is the flighteft and moft tranfitory imaginable; and, generally, as foon as we have left the room, vanifhes, and is gone for ever.

It is upon account of this dull fenfibility to the afflictions of others, that magnanimity amidft great diftrefs appears always fo divinely graceful. He appears to be more than mortal, who can fupport the moft dreadful calamities. We are amazed to find that he can command himfelf fo entirely. His firmnefs, at the fame time, perfectly coincides with our infenfibility. There is the moft perfect correfpondence between his fentiments and ours, and upon that account the moft perfect propriety in his behaviour. We wonder at that ftrength of mind which is capable of fo noble and generous an effort; and this, fentiment of complete fympathy and approbation, mixed and animated with wonder and furprife, conftitutes what is properly called admiration.

Cato, furrounded on all fides by his enemies, unable to refift them, difdaining to fubmit to them, and reduced,

neduced, by the proud maxims of that age, to the
neceffity of deftroying himfelf; yet, never fhrinking;
from his misfortunes, never fupplicating, with the la-
mentable voice of wretchednefs, thofe miferable, fympathetic tears, which we are always fo unwilling to
give; but, on the contrary, arming himfelf with
manly fortitude, and, the moment before he executes
his fatal refolution, giving, with his ufual tranquility,
all neceffary orders for the fafety of his friends, appears to Seneca, that great preacher of infenfibility,
a fpectacle, which even the gods themfelves might
behold with pleafure and admiration.

Whenever we meet, in common life, with any examples of fuch heroic magnanimity, we are always
extremely affected. We are more apt to weep and
fhed tears for fuch as, in this manner, feem to feel
nothing for themfelves, than for thofe who give way
to all the weaknefs of forrow; and, in this particular cafe, the fympathetic grief of the fpectator appears to go beyond the original paffion, in the perfon
principally concerned. The friends of Socrates all
wept when he drank the laft baneful potion, while he
himfelf expreffed the gayeft and moft cheerful tranquility.

Upon all fuch occafions the fpectator makes no effort in order to conquer his fympathetic forrow. He
is under no fear that it will tranfport him to any
thing that is extravagant and improper; he is rather pleafed with the fenfibility of his own heart, and
gives way to it with complacence and felf-appro-
bation.

On the contrary, he always appears, in fome meafure, mean and defpicable, who is funk in forrow and
dejection upon account of any calamity of his own.
We cannot bring ourfelves to feel for him, what he
feels for himfelf, and what, perhaps, we fhould feel
for ourfelves, if in his fituation; we therefore defpife
him;

him ; unjuftly perhaps, if any fentiment could
be regarded as unjuft, to which we are by nature ir-
refiftibly determined. How did it difgrace the memory of the intrepid Duke of Biron, who had fo oft-
en braved death in the field, that he wept upon the
fcaffold, when he beheld the ftate to which he was
fallen ; and remembered the favour and the glory from
which his own rafhnefs had fo unfortunately thrown
him !

——— ◦◦◦ ———

MARIUS,
OR,
THE ABUSE OF RICHES :
A CHARACTER TAKEN FROM LIFE.

MARIUS is a man of a very extenfive fortune, of
opulent connexions, and poffeffed of health, talents,
and every comfort that Fortune, as fhe is called, can
beftow upon man : his wife is allowed to be one of
the moft beautiful, accomplifhed, and amiable women
in England. Marius therefore feems apparently to
think himfelf too happy, and in order to familiar-
ize his mind with misfortune, has connected himfelf
with a woman of the ftage, poffeffed indeed of fome
beauty, but without one fpark of honour, generofity,
or tendernefs.

On this woman Marius fquanders immenfe fums,
without even obtaining her affections ; fhe receives
the price of her interviews with the coolnefs of a
common bargain of trade, and defpifes her cuftomer
at heart ; nay infults him to his face, and in the prefence of others ; but he yet doats upon her, and unlefs that ficklenefs of tafte which is peculiar to men
of gallantry, comes to his relief, he will probably
impair his health and fortune in her fervice. Are
thefe acts of a wife man ? Are men happy in pro-

portion as they are rich*? But Marius is not a fingular character. Hundreds every day give proof that if riches confer happinefs, it is a happinefs of which they are heartily tired, and of which they ftrive to get rid by the quickeft poffible means. And after every confideration of this fubject, it will be found that the ufe of riches, as of every other poffeffion, confifts in moderation.

Lefs than moderation is niggardlinefs ; more is intemperance. The one narrows and confines the heart, the other corrupts and pollutes it.

------⟡⟡------

A WALK IN BEDLAM HOSPITAL.
BY A LADY.

Some of the lunatics I obferved were playing at cards, whilft numbers were walking about, eating their dinners in clean wooden bowls, very contented and cheerful. One of this clafs much urged me to partake with him. His appearance and behaviour retained much of the gentleman ; amidft his wanderings he was very polite, but uneafy under reftraint. He faid, he was ufed very ill to be put under confinement, for which no one gave him a reafon ; therefore, he urged us to procure his enlargement, by application to fome perfons of diftinction and power, to whom he would give us an addrefs. I inquired the caufe of this lively captive's being in durance, and learned he was a victim to ill-fated love !

At our entrance among the *female* patients (where no man was permitted to attend us) I addreffed myfelf to a well-looking matron, and admiring the neatnefs

----

* Wealth never can *true* happinefs procure :
Contented minds are happy tho' they're poor.

nefs of her drefs, which was a black taffeta pinned back, fhe told me, filks of that texture were fo conftantly hitching here and there, that fhe chofe to make a fuit of clothes of it at once, and then it was a court day always. I had converfed with this lady but a few minutes, before fhe difcovered the provincial dialect of the company, and afked for feveral families in Gloucefter-fhire. This being a lucid interval with feveral ; another lunatic argued very calmly, that fhe was not mad, but confined to make her fo, that fome near relation of her's might take poffeffion of her fortune and eftate. But if thofe vifitors, who faw her in that difmal manfion, had one fpark of benevolence, humanity, or pity warming their bofoms ; fhe conjured us, by all that was good and facred, to ufe the means fhe pointed out, with feeming reafon, to procure her liberty. She extorted the promife fhe fo ardently defired ; and then, with an awful folemnity, She added, "God was juft ; and if we did not religioufly keep the promife made to her, might vengeance purfue the violators, and all the thunder-bolts of heaven defcend on our heads ; for fhe was Jove's wife, and Jupiter had undone her. Pride and romantic notions, which dethrone reafon, and deftroy human happinefs, I found had a great fhare in turning the brains of this fuppofed goddefs.

Thefe likewife ufurped a powerful fway in the next object I turned to, who was a lady that fancied herfelf an *emprefs*. I made my court to her by offering my fnuff-box, as I found a fmall paper of fnuff had been a more acceptable prefent to each individual before, than the freedom of the city, or a purfe of gold could poffibly have been. This Utopian queen, with her paper crown and fupercilious air however, did me the honour to take a pinch of fnuff from me ; but had fhe held out the fceptre of

royalty

royalty, she could not have seemed to have confer-
red a greater dignity on me, than by the extension of
her hand.

Conversation seemed a reviving cordial to most of
the other female patients, who were solicitous to engage me in it, according to their different turns of
mind, or diforders, in which they showed the influence their religion and country had over them. The
Roman Catholics mourned I was not fluent in the
French language, and that I could not difcoufe of
their blessed Lady, the Virgin Mary, nor any of their
holy faints.

The last person I conversed with in these gloomy
walls, asked me if I was acquainted with Mr. John Wes-
ly, the preacher? On my answering I knew him, the
sweet creature said, she had been crucified to him *ten*
years; and his cross was easy to bear. I then asked
her the reason of her confinement? She very serene-
ly replied, that her husband and two pretty babes
died last Christmas, and her cruel brother would
not let her take leave of either, but had the coffins
nailed up without letting her take one parting kiss!
" And you know, Madam," said the poor distressed
object, (her bofom heaving with maternal fighs, and
her eyes imploring pity!) " I could not follow the
corpse of my dear Charles, and our sweet children,
like a cow lowing for her calf."

I could not help smiling at her expressions, though
I lamented in thought, that this combat of religion
and natural affection, which are in themfelves fo
pure, should have been too strong for the intellects
of this amiable innocent, which I found to be the case;
for she seemed to intimate, God would have no rivals
in the hearts of those he fanctified, and therefore
took her husband and children from her; but she
should affuredly go to heaven to them, and meet to
part no more; and there she earnestly wished to

meet

meet me, a wifh I fincerely joined in ; but was o-
bliged to give her fome hope of feeing me once more
on earth firft, as fhe entreated me to vifit her again,
and to remember how faft we are all haftening out of
this world, and to be prepared for the next.

I left the women's ward with her fervent blefling,
and quitted Bedlam, fully convinced of the truth of a
common obfervation ; That there are many more mad
perfons out of it, than in it.

RELIGION THE SOURCE OF HAPPINESS.

Defire not riches, they Bewitch :---
Contentment makes the poor man rich.

THE covetequs man, never fatisfied with adding
houfe to houfe, field to field, and thoufand to thoufand, is a glaring proof that happinefs is not obtained by riches, nor content purchafed by abundance ;
the facred records affure us, riches take themfelves
wings, and flee away like an eagle towards heaven ;
the young man in the Gofpel thought himfelf a happy man with the poffeffion of the wealth of this
world, till Chrift informed him of the neceffity of parting with all, if he would attain eternal life ; indeed,
if we look around us, and obferve the actions of the
major part of mankind, we fhall find wealth the goal
they are daily running to, the mark they are conftantly fhooting at, or the foundation on which they
vainly imagine felicity is built. But the grand miftake of the multitude lies, in taking the fhadow for
the fubftance, and following an *ignis fatuus* inftead of
the light of truth.

Let the fober and difcerning man be afked what is
happinefs, or wherein does it confift ? and he will anfwer, in the tranquil poffeffion of a contented mind ;—
yes,

Yes, it muſt be ſo, or whence is it, that we ſo often ſee the laborious hind cheerful, though a ſtranger to rich-es, and barely maintained by his daily toil ? It is not affluence ; it is not honours ; it is not dignity or re-nown, that conſtitute or can procure *true* happineſs ; no, they are utterly inſufficient, even though accom-panied with all the dazzling ſplendor of nobility and parade, to procure eaſe under trouble, comfort in afflidion, or ſupport in the views of death. *Religion* alone, as Dr. YOUNG very juſtly ſays, in his Night Thoughts,

> Amid life's pains, abaſements, emptineſs,
> The ſoul can comfort, elevate, and fill.

G. W.

A FRIENDLY ADMONITION,
TO
EVERY READER.

Retire ; the world ſhut out ; thy thoughts call home.

Dr. YOUNG.

IN the midſt of the hurries and buſtle of trade and merchandiſe, ſurrounded with a thouſand objeds to engage the attention, and conſtantly employed in pur-ſuit of the things of time and ſenſe, what more ſeaſon-able and important admonition can be given to the wealthy merchant and induſtrious tradeſman, than that which is held out and contained in the motto I have choſen as above, from Dr. Young's Night Thoughts ?

Retire ! yes, it is the duty of every ſon and daugh-ter of Adam to retire ; but you may aſk, *For* what, *from* what, and *when* muſt I retire ? I anſwer *From* the common concerns of life, to inquire how matters ſtand between God and the ſoul, *every evening,* before you retire to reſt. **C**   To

To be wholly fwallowed up in the affairs and bufinefs of *this* world, without a thought on, and much
lefs preparation for, another and better world beyond
the grave, feems to me very impolitic, to fay the leaft
of it ; but it is the cafe of too many, even profeffors of
religion, in the prefent day ; if they can but make
themfelves mafters of the mammon of unrighteouf-
nefs, and become the fons of fortune ; little, if any
care is taken to be rich in good works ; lefs concern,
if poffible, felt about the future well-being of the immortal foul ; and no thought at all inculcated, refpecting the grand and important point of the end of man's
creation, and the means to attain it.   If this is the cafe,
our being called Chriftians is only a burlefque upon
Chriftianity, and our profeffions of religion only hypocrify and deception.

G. W.

<hr>

THE
BENEFITS of CHRISTIAN PATIENCE
UNDER
GREAT DISTRESS.

Thy will, O God! not mine, be done.

CHRISTIAN patience is allowed to be the univerfal panacea under inevitable misfortunes ; It has a
wonderful efficacy to ftrengthen and fupport the mind,
whilft it rectifies the judgment, and removes from the
eye that falfe glare, through which it was wont to
view the objects of fenfe.

We are directed by it, to converfe with the great Father of Spirits, which elevates the foul above the fenfe
of human diftrefs.   At fuch a time, it is a confolatory
thought to meditate on what the Saviour of the world
fuffered when on earth ; how he left the bofom of his
Father, and the right hand of glory, in the celeftial

mansions,

manfions, to endure the complicated diftrefs of pain, penury, and reproach, to redeem us from fin, milery, and woe.

I have been vifiting the manfions of poverty and difeafe, which has given my thoughts a very ferious turn. This day have I feen a divine cf eminent learning, who was lately held in high efteem, now funk by the power of oppreffion and refentment, to abfolute penury, without a fhilling for fupport, and attacked by a complication of diforders, which renders the unhappy object unable to do any thing to alleviate his diftrefs.

This is a fcene which draws very hard upon humanity ; and thofe perfons who bafk in affluence, and never turn their feet to the habitations of mifery, nor their ear to its complaints, can have but little idea what their fellow-creatures fuffer, whofe delicacy cf fituation will not permit them to be common beggars.

Well might Job fay, Man is born to trouble as the fparks fly upward ; for dangers meet him at his firft entrance into life, and he enters into it crying, which implies pain : and no fooner doth he commence an actor on the tranfitory ftage, than he is fubject to innumerable impending evils ; which are often the harbingers of that real grief, which bedews his way with tears, from the cradle to grave. Nor can infant innocence, youthful vivacity, manly ftrength, fapient age, nor yet the benign fmiles of an earthly prince, fecure the man from that numerous train of evils incident to mortality.

------◦◦◦------

VIRTUE, MAN's HIGHEST INTEREST.
A SOLILOQUY.

I FIND myfelf exifting upon a little fpot, furrounded every way by an immenfe and unknown expanfion.

Where

Where am I ? What fort of place do I inhabit ? Is it exactly accommodated in every inftance to my convenience ? is there no excefs of cold, none of heat, to offend me ? Am I never annoyed by animals, either of my own kind or a different ? Is every thing fubfervient to me, as though I had ordered all myfelf ? No, nothing like it, the fartheft from it poffible. The world appears not, then, originally made for the private convenience of me alone ?. It does not. But is it not poffible fo to accommodate it, by my own particular induftry ?. If to accommodate man and beaft, heaven and earth, if this be out of my power, it is not poffible. What confequences then follows ? or can there be any other than this ? If I feek an intereft of my own detached from that of others, I feek an intereft which is chimerical, and can never have exiftence.

How then muft I determine ? Have I no intereft at all ? If I have not, I am a fool for ftaying here : It is a fmoky houfe, and the fooner out of it the better. But why no intereft ? Can I be contented with none but one feparate and detached ? Is a focial intereft, joined with others, fuch an abfurdity as not to be admitted ? The bee, the beaver, and all the tribes of herding animals, are enough to convince me that the thing is fomewhere at leaft poffible. How, then, am I affured that it is not equally true of man ? Admit it : and what follows ; If fo, then, honour and juftice are my intereft ; then the whole train of moral virtues are my intereft ; without fome portion of which, not even thieves can maintain fociety.

But, farther ftill ; I ftop not here ; I purfue this focial intereft as far as I can trace my feveral relations. I pafs from my own ftock, my own neighbourhood, my own nation, to the whole race of mankind, as difperfed throughout the earth. Am I not related to
                                                    them

them all, by the mutual aids of commerce, by the general intercourse of arts and letters, and by that common nature of which we all participate?

Again, I must have food and clothing. Without a proper genial warmth, I instantly perish. Am I not related, in this view, to the very earth itself? to the distant sun, from whose beams I derive vigour? and to that stupendous course and order of the infinite hosts of heaven, by which the times and seasons ever uniformly pass on? Were this order once confounded, I should not probably survive a moment, so absolutely do I depend on this common general welfare. What, then, have I to do, but to enlarge virtue into piety? Not only honour and justice, and what I owe to man, is my interest; but gratitude also, acquiescence, resignation, adoration, and all I owe to this great polity, and its great Governor, our common parent.

> Virtue alone is happiness below ;
> And all our knowledge is—ourselves to know. POPE,

VIRTUE ENFORCED ON ALL,
FROM THE
HOPES AND FEARS OF A FUTURE STATE.

TO imprefs mankind with a lively and deep perfuation that a vicious life will most certainly lead to eternal misery, and the opposite to eternal happiness in another state and world, cannot be too frequently made a topic with those, whose peculiar office it is to set forth the great truths of religion.

How did my soul rejoice within me, on hearing our curate the other day expatiate on the joys of futurity! The happiness of heaven, he said, is beyond any thing we can conceive in this state of imperfection. It is a felicity not only perfect in degree, but perpetual in duration. As it is a perfect felicity, it

must

muſt be the moſt refined, and ſpiritual : It muſt con-
fiſt in the extenſion of our knowledge, and ſublima-
tion of our love.   Our underſtandings will be enlarged and enlightened with a brighter diſplay of the
divine perfections, with a clearer knowledge of the
divine works, in the wonders of creation, of providence, of grace—while, united in the bonds of indiſ-
ſoluble friendſhip, and glowing with the ardours of ſe-
raphic love, we ſhall participate with the heavenly
choir in ſwelling the ſong of unceaſing gratitude, a-
doration, and praiſe to the eternal Fountain and Author of all happineſs.   At the ſame time, while ab-
ſorbed in this delightful employment, we ſhall inſen-
ſibly grow into a reſemblance of the Deity—We
ſhall ſee God, and we ſhall be like Him.   And can
greater happineſs be conceived, than to be like
Him who is the inexhauſtible ſource of felicity and
perfection ? ʻ

Beſides, in the preſence of God (he continued) there
is not only fulneſs of joy, but pleaſures for ever-
more.   Indeed, without the addition of an *eternal*
duration, the ſum of the heavenly felicity muſt be
deficient.

It muſt ſtrike a damp on the joys of the bleſſed,
to think a time, however remote, was fixed for
the period of them.   And the more exalted their
happineſs were, this thought would give proportiona-
ble pain.

Divine wiſdom, therefore, hath ſo ordained—that
while the falſe and empty delights of this world are
temporary and tranſient, the truer and more ſub-
ſtantial pleaſures of the other ſhould be permanent,
as they are excellent—and that heaven ſhould not
only be an exceeding but an *eternal* weight of glory
—to poſſeſs the mind with a full and complete felicity.

Again, how was I ſhocked with horror when the
ſame.

fame preacher reverfed the picture, and proceeded to defcribe the torments of the damned! "Their mifery," he obferved, "will principally confift in an exclufion from the blifsful prefence of God. They fhall have a *diftant* fight, indeed, of the heavenly world, but it will be a fight in the fame fituation the rich man in the Gofpel faw Paradife—with an impaffible gulph between! A fight that muft ferve only to inflame their felf-condemnation, their difappointment, and defpair!

"Their mifery will further confift (he added) in a remorfe of confcience; arifing from reflections on their paft lives—their bafe ingratitude to God—their obftinate folly, and perverfenefs—intimated by the fcripture expreffion of the worm that never dieth. A worm that will prey upon their minds, with an infinitely keener anguifh, than a worm preys on our mortal flefh. Inftead of the pleafures refulting from extended knowledge, from the endearing enjoyments of the pureft love, the tendereft friendfhips, and the fublime raptures of praife and adoration which ever agitate the bofoms of the bleffed; the accurfed fhall know more, only to be more miferable; and by the exercife of the moft diabolical paffions, of envy, hatred, malice, and revenge, fhall only ftrive more and more to aggravate each other's torment. This, added to that blacknefs of darknefs, or the flames of that fire that fhall never be quenched, to which they are doomed—muft conftitute a mifery fufficiently dreadful. A mifery, however, ftill imbittered by the ingredient—its eternal duration. *Eternal!* how muft this thought fharpen the edge of the fufferings, and heap up the meafure of infernal woe!

HUMANITY.

HUMANITY AND BENEVOLENCE;

AN·ADDRESS TO YOUTH.

YOUTH is the proper feafon for cultivating the benevolent and humane affections. As a great part of your happinefs is to depend on the connexions which you form with others, it is of highimportance that you acquire betimes the temper and the manners which will render fuch connexions comfortable. Let a fenfe of juftice be the foundation of all your focial qualities.

Engrave on your mind that facred rule, of " doing in all things to others according as you wifh that they fhould do unto you." For this end, imprefs your-felves with a deep fenfe of the original and natural e-quality of men. Whatever advantages of birth or fortune you poffefs, never difplay them with an often-tatious fuperiority. Leave the fubordinations of rank, to regulate the intercourfe of more advanced years. At prefent it becomes you to act among your companions as man with man.

Remember how unknown to you are the viciffitudes of the world ; and how often they, on whom igno-rant and contemptuous young men once looked down with fcorn, have rifen to be their fuperiors in future years. Compaffion is an emotion of which you ought never to be afhamed. Graceful in youth is the tear of fympathy, and the heart that melts at the tale of woe.

Let not eafe and indulgence contract your affec-tions, and wrap you up in felfifh enjoyment. Ac-cuftom yourfelves to think of the diftreffes of hu-man life ; of the folitary cottage, the dying pa-rent, and the weeping orphan. Never fport with pain and diftrefs in any of your amufements, nor treat even the meaneft infect with wanton cru-elty.

NERVOUS

NERVOUS COMPLAINTS
THE
EFFECTS OF LUXURY.

Luxurious indolence generates difeafes.

IT is reafonable to fuppofe that the mind is fimilar to the body, and influenced according as we exercife it ; thus exertion of the body will give it ftrength, and exercifing our judgment and memory will add to our ftock of ideas, and form a pleafure not to be tafted by an ignorant barbarian.

Nervous complaints are more frequent in what we call civilized countries, and where luxuries are introduced, than in thofe where the fuperfluities of life are not fo abundant, and in every country more among the *rich* than the lower claffes of people ; for where the principal care of a man's life confifts in finding means to fupport himfelf and his family, he is always engaged in a pleafing attention, and there is but little time for the introduction of any other care on his mind than his daily employ ; which, if laborious, enfures him health, and makes the bed of repofe on which he refts his fatigued limbs, one of the principal comforts of his life* ; if there happens to be a day on which he refrains from his ufual exertions, he enjoys the pleafures of fatiety ; and even a little idlenefs, as being a novelty, pleafes him.

Let us confider another character, a man who enjoys an ample fortune : He may be fuppofed to make himfelf happy with the idea that there are a number of mechanics and fervants who are ready, for pay, to provide any object or pleafure which his fancy

---

* The fleep of a labouring man is fweet.
ECCLESIASTES, V, 12.

fancy may dictate; fo far from merely fatisfying thofe defires which Nature intended he fhould poffefs for the purpofe of maintaining life and propagating his fpecies, he is pleafed with any invention which can give a poignancy to his daily food ; and ftudies every means to gratify his luft, and give a double relifh to every kind of enjoyment, till at length his mind can only be charmed by every fpecies of luxury ; his fenfes and appetites being repeatedly abufed by too frequent a repetition of what can give them pleafure, become in fome meafure callous, and at certain times lofe their capability of receiving fatisfaction.

The rich man finds himfelf liftlefs, and complaint of lownefs of fpirits, which complaint is generally termed nervous. In fuch cafes the bottle is frequently had recourfe to, which intoxicates the mind and gives a *temporary* flow of fpirits ; a fubfequent lownefs is the confequence, which renders neceffary a repetition of the intoxicating draught ; and thus a habit of drinking is eftablifhed, which brings on many nervous and chronic difeafes, and eventually deftroys the beft conftitutions.

APPROVED MAXIMS.

WORTHY REMEMBRANCE AND REGARD.

HYPOCRICY is a homage that vice pays to virtue.

Every man, however little, makes a figure in his *own* eyes.

Self-partiality hides from us thofe very faults in ourfelves, which we fee and blame in others.

The injuries we do, and thofe we fuffer, are feldom weighed in the fame balance.

Men generally put a greater value on the favours they beftow, than on thofe they receive.   He

He who is puffed up with the firft gale of profperi-ty, will bend beneath the firft blaft of adverfity.

Examine well the counfels that favours your de-fires.

The pomp which diftinguifhes the great man from the mob, defends him not from a fever nor from grief.

The fmalleft prick of a nail, the flighteft paffion of the foul, is capable of rendering infipid the monarchy of the world.

Narrow minds think nothing right that is above their own capacity.

Thofe who are the moft faulty, are the moft prone to find faults in others.

To be angry is to punifh myfelf for the fault of a-nother.

The moft profitable revenge, the moft rational, and the moft pleafant, is to make it the intereft of the injuriòus perfon not to hurt you a fecond time.

Be moderate in your pleafures, that your relifh for them may continue.

Solicitude in hiding failings makes them appear the greater. It is a fafer and eafier courfe frankly to ac-knowledge them. A man owns that he is ignorant: We admire his modefty. He fays he is old: We fcarce think him fo. He declares himfelf poor: We do not be-lieve it.

To gain knowledge of ourfelves, the beft way is to convert the imperfections of others into a mirror for difcovering our own.

Apply yourfelf more to acquire knowledge than to fhow it. Men commonly take great pains to put off the little ftock they have ; but they take little pains to acquire more.

If you would teach fecrecy to others, begin with yourfelf. How can you expect another will keep your fecret, when you yourfelf cannot ?   To

To deal with a man you muſt know his temper, by which you can lead him ; or his ends, by which you can purſuade him ; or his friends, by whom you can govern him.

The firſt ingredient in converſation is truth ; the next, good ſenſe ; the third, good humour ; the laſt, wit.

To be an Engliſhman in London, a Frenchman in Paris, a Spaniard in Madrid, is no eaſy matter ; and yet it is neceſſary.

He who cannot bear a jeſt ought never to make one.

RURAL FELICITY.
A FRAGMENT.

Sweet are the pleaſures of a rural life.

MANY are the ſilent and unenvied pleaſures of the honeſt peaſant, who riſes cheerfully to his ruſtic labour. Look into his dwelling, where the ſcene of every man's happineſs chiefly lies : He has the ſame domeſtic endearments, as much joy and comfort in his children, and as flattering hopes of their doing well, to enliven his hours and gladden his heart, as you could conceive in the moſt affluent ſtation ; and I make no doubt but if the true account of his joys and ſufferings were to be balanced with thoſe of his betters, that the upſhot would prove to be little more than this ; that the rich man had the more meat, but the poor man the better ſtomach ; the one had more luxury, more able phyſicians to attend and ſet him to rights ; the other, more health and ſoundneſs in his bones, and leſs occaſion for their help ; that, after theſe two articles betwixt them were balanced, in all other things they ſtood upon a level ; that the

fun

fun, shines as warm, the air blows as fresh, and the earth breaths as fragrant upon the one as the other ; and that they have an *equal* share in all the beauties and real benefits of nature.

> A bed of flow'rs, a grove, a level plain,
> A rising hill, a field of golden grain ;
> A lowly cottage more true pleasure brings,
> Than pomp can furnish in the courts of kings,
> It needs no toil to find the way to bliss ;
> Who makes *content* his guide, can never miss :
> No lofty walls this heav'nly flower embrace,
> All wild it grows, and blooms in every place.

THE SELF-TORMENTOR ;

A CHARACTER TAKEN FROM LIFE.

A YOUNG fellow, who stands in the relationship of cousin-german to me, is what may justly be termed a constitutional self-tormentor. For he was so even from his infancy. When a school-boy, whatever was in another's possession he always considered better than his own. His top never spun so well, nor his marbles rolled so dexterously, as those of his companions. His task was always harder than any body else's, and his repetition of it listened to with prejudiced ears by our master.

On entering into life, this strange humour increased upon him. He conceived every dinner he was not a partaker of, much more excellent than the one in which he participated. Every taylor, if he changed a dozen times a month, was smarter than those he employed : and every estate he heard of, happier

D   situated

fituated and better improved than his own, though the rents were much inferior to what he was in the receipt of.

He attached himfelf to a fine accomplifhed girl, but foon found out that her fifter was much more charming. This fifter had a young friend, who had as much the advantage of her, and that friend a relation that furpaffed them all. His ftrange humour foon marked him for an object of contempt ; and however, out of refpect to his family, he is to this day received in fome few houfes ; he is tolerated but not *approved ;* and pitied but not *honoured ;* notwithftanding his *birth, education,* and large *eftate.*

MATRIMONIAL INFIDELITY
ACCOUNTED FOR.

AN ESSAY.

LORD A. marries Mifs B. becaufe fhe has a good fortune, and fhe weds his lordfhip for a *title.* The honey-moon paft, feparate beds take place ; they feldom meet but at meals, and then fcarce recollect the ceremony was ever faid ; and if they do, it is only to upbraid one another upon the authority of being man and wife. This difagreeable *tete-a-tete* being over, he flies to the arms of his miftrefs, to find that confolation his wife could not afford him ; and, probably, by way of *lex talionis,* fhe goes to meet her *Cifcifbeo.* If her ladyfhip's fortune is nearly exhaufted, and his lordfhip has another rich heirefs in view, he may probably fue for *crim. con.* to obtain a divorce. If not, he winks at her infidelity, and is very well pleafed to think, he has a *locum tenens* to take all matrimonial drudgery off his hands ; and thus by a

kind

kind of tacit compact, they may continue in a state of adultery for fome years, without ever upbraiding each other upon this fcore.

Again, Lord C. marries Lady D. on the fcore of family alliance and connexion. Lord C. a perfect emaciated macaroni, Lady D. a woman of fpirit, vigor, and paffions, finds herfelf deceived in her hufband, and that fhe might as well have married one of Rackftrow's dolls. Thus difappointed, in the very prime of life, when the pulfe beats high, and the blood circulates with juvenile warmth through every vein; may we not fuppofe that opportunity and importunity, in a man worthy of her embraces, may feduce her from the riged path of virtue, and make her yield to a flame, kindled by nature and fanned by inclination*? The lady cannot, it is true, be vindicated, according to the nice rules of chaftity and honour; but I think her *nominal* hufband can have but little reafon to complain; efpecially, if we find him nightly wallowing in the ftews of corruption, in the arms of profligate harlots, to gratify an imaginary paffion, which his whims and caprices, fuited to the place, can only awaken.

Once more. The Duke of E. weds a moft amiable woman, on whom he thinks he has fixed his affections, and fhe entertains the higheft efteem for him. For fome time they live in a ftate of connubial felicity, and when he might fay with the poet,

Whilft in the circle of her arms I lay,

Whole fummers funs roll'd unperceiv'd away;

I years for days, I days for moments told;

And was furpris'd to find that I grew old.

Se

Youth and *Age*, or *December* and *May*, will ever be a contraft, particularly in the *marriage* ftate, which, upon rational principles, can never be happily reconciled.

So far a fucceffion of happy months have rolled; but now, whether from fatiety, or natural propenfity, his favourite amufements preponderate againft domeftic felicity. Horfes, hounds, and the turf, have more charms than the animated Venus de Medicis. Days, weeks, nay *months* elapfe, whilft the fair Miranda is forgotten for a fox-chace, or fweepftakes. Thefe gloomy intervals fhe muft fill up with cards, routs, and coquetry—fatal rocks, which too many thought-lefs females have fplit upon.

Abfence and neglect on the one hand, affiduities and purfuit on the other, will probably create a ri-val, and fupprefs all thofe virtuous fcruples, from a breaft that never meant to deviate from honour.— But as fhe has a potent rival in Chloe, or Cleopatra (on account of their fleetnefs) fo his Grace finds one in Capt. Fairface, and at his return difcovers as much coolnefs in her Grace, as fhe experienced in him, during a *fix* weeks abfence.

If fuch caufes as thefe do not in fome meafure pal-liate the crime of female infidelity, they at leaft ac-count for it. And I am fo far convinced of the na-tural good difpofition of my fair countrywomen, that I will venture to pronounce, not one in a hundred, I might fay in a thoufand, would go aftray, if it was not for the unkind behaviour of their hufbands. Let thefe ftrive to merit the affections of their wives, and there will (I doubt not) be few, if any, complaints of matrimonial infidelities.

THE-

THE HYPOCRITE;

A

PICTURE TAKEN FROM LIFE

Beware of Hypocrites.

HE who appears a faint, that he may with greater safety act as a devil, is, in my opinion, the worst of sinners. There can be no excuse for him ; he cannot even say with the generality of offenders, I erred through ignorance, for I knew not what I did.

I once knew a man who would frequently disburse considerable sums of money in building churches, and other public acts of charity, where fame might be acquired ; and yet, if merit in distrefs privately sued to him for relief, he was always so necessitated, he had not wherewithal to help them.

I knew another who starved his family, denied them common necessaries of life, and preached up mortification for the good of their souls ; yet would he himself partake of every thing voluptuous, at other men's cost.

His never-ending harangue was that of abusing mankind openly ; lashing their vices, or follies, in the most ill-natured, gross, foul-mouthed, and ungenerous manner ; yet would he fawn, cringe, flatter, and meanly sue for favours from those above him.

Here was ostentation, pride, self-esteem, luxury, avarice, impudence, deceit, and the highest degree of ill-nature, all cloaked under the sanctified pretence of true piety.

THE

FOLLY OF INCONSISTENT EXPECTATIONS.

THIS world may be confidered as a great mart of commerce, where fortune expofes to our view various commodities ; *riches, eafe, tranquility, fame, integrity, knowledge,* &c.

Every thing is marked at a fettled price. Our time, our labour, our ingenuity, is fo much ready money which we are to lay out to the beft advantage. Examine, compare, chufe, reject, but ftand to your own judgment ; and do not, like children, when you have purchafed one thing, repine that you do not poffefs another which you did not purchafe.

Such is the force of well-regulated induftry, that a fteady and vigorous exertion of our faculties, directed to one end, will generally enfure fuccefs. Would you, for inftance, be rich ? Do you think that fingle point worth the facrificing every thing elfe to ? You may then be rich. Thoufands have become fo from the loweft beginnings, by toil, patient diligence, and attention to the minuteft articles of expence and profit. But you muft give up the pleafures of leifure, of a vacant mind, and of a free unfufpicious temper.

" But I cannot fubmit to drudgery like this, I feel a fpirit above it." It is well ; be above it then ; only do not repine that you are not rich.

Is knowledge the pearl of great price ? That too, may be purchafed by fteady application, and long folitary hours of ftudy and reflection. Beftow thefe, and you fhall be learned.

You are a modeft man, you love quiet and independence, and have a delicacy and referve in your temper which renders it impoffible for you to elbow your way in the world, and be the herald of your own merits. Be content, then, with a modeft retirement,
with

with the efteem of a few intimate friends, with the praifes of a blamelefs heart, and a delioate ingenuous fpirit and difpofition ; but refign the fplendid diftinctions of the world to thofe who can better fcramble for them.

------◄◊►◄◊►------

PICTURESQUE DESCRIPTION
OF THE
VALE OF KESWICK, IN CUMBERLAND.

INSTEAD of the narrow flip of valley which is feen at Dovedale, you have at Kefwick a vaft amphitheatre, in circumference above twenty miles. Inftead of a meagre rivulet, a noble living lake, ten miles round, of an oblong form, adorned with a variety of wooded iflands. . The rocks indeed of Dovedale are finely wild, pointed, and irregular ; but the hills are both little and unanimated ; and the margin of the brook is poorly edged with weeds, morafs, and brufhwood. But at Kefwick, you will, on one fide of the lake, fee a rich and beautiful landfcape of cultivated fields, rifing to the eye in fine inequalities, with noble groves of oak, happily difperfed, and climbing the adjacent hills, fhade above fhade, in the moft various and picturefqe forms. On the oppofite fhore, you will find rocks and cliffs of ftupendous height, hanging broken over the lake in horrible grandeur, fome of them a *thoufand* fect high, the woods climbing up their fteep and fhaggy fides, where mortal foot has never yet approached.

On thefe dreadful heights the eagles build their nefts ; a variety of water-falls are feen pouring from their fummits, and tumbling in vaft fheets from rock to rock in rude and terrible magnificence. While all.

all fides of this immence amphitheatre the lofty mountains rife around, piercing the very clouds, in fhapes
as fpiry and fantaftic as the rocks of Dovedale.

To this I muft add the frequent and bold projec-
tion of the cliffs into the lake, forming noble bays and
promontories.   In other parts they finely retire from
it, and often open in abrupt chafms or clefts, through
which at hand you fee rich and cultivated vales ; and
beyond thefe, at various diftances, mountain rifing o-
ver mountain ; among which, new profpects prefent
themfelves in a mift, till the eye is loft in an agreeable perplexity.

The natural variety of colouring which the feveral
objects produce, is no lefs wonderful and pleafing ;
the ruling tincts in the vallies being thofe of azure,
green, and gold ; yet ever various, arifing from an
intermixture of the lake; the woods, the grafs, and
cornfields.   Thefe are finely contrafted by the gray
rocks and cliffs ; and the whole heightened by the
yellow ftreams of light, the purple hues and mifty
azure of the mountains.

Sometimes a ferene air and clear fky difclofe the
tops of the higheft hills ; at other times, you fee the
clouds involving their fummits, refting on their fides,
or defcending to their bafe, and rolling among the
vallies, as in a vaft furnace.   When the winds are
high, they roar among the cliffs and caverns like
peals of thunder ; then, too, the clouds are feen in
vaft bodies fweeping along the hills in gloomy greatnefs, while the lake joins the tumult, and toffes like a
fea.   But in calm weather, the whole fcene becomes
new : the lake is a perfect mirror, and the landfcape
in all its beauty : iflands, fields, woods, rocks, and
mountains, are feen inverted, and floating on its fur-
face.

I will now carry you to the top of a cliff, where,
if you dare approach the ridge, a new fcene of aftonifhment

the ment prefents itfelf; where the valley, lake, and iflands, feem lying at your feet; where this expanfe of water appears diminifhed to a little pool, amidft the vaft and immeafurable objects that furround it; for the fummits of more diftant hills appear beyond thofe you have already feen : and, rifing behind each other in fucceffive ranges and azure groupes of crag- gy and broken fteeps, form an immenfe and awful picture, which can only be expreffed by the image of a tempeftuous fea of mountains.

Let me now conduct you down again to the val- ley, and conclude with one circumftance more— which is, that a walk by ftill moon-light (at which time the diftant water-falls are heard in all their va- riety of found) among thefe enchanting dales, opens fuch fcenes of delicate beauty, repofe, and folemnity, as exceed all defcription.

RESIGNATION TO PROVIDENCE RECOMMENDED,

AS THE DUTY OF ALL.

THE darts of adverfe fortune are always levelled at our heads. Some reach us ; fome graze againft us, and fly to wound our neighbours. Let us there- fore impofe an equal temper on our minds, and pay without murmuring the tribute which we owe to hu- manity : the winter brings cold, and we muft freeze ; the fummer returns with heat, and we muft melt : the inclemency of the air diforders our health, and we muft be fick. Here we are expofed to wild beafts, and there to men more favage than the beafts. And if we efcape the inconveniences and dangers of the air and earth, there are perils by water and perils by fire.   This

This eftablifhed courfe of things it is not in our power to change; but it is in our power to affume fuch a greatnefs of mind as becomes wife and virtuous men; as may enable us to encounter the accidents of life with fortitude, and to conform ourfelves to the order of Nature, who governs her great kingdom, the world, by continual mutations.

Let us fubmit ourfelves to this order; let us be perfuaded that whatever does happen, *ought* to happen, and never be fo foolifh as to expoftulate with Nature. The beft refolution we can take is, to fuffer with patience what we cannot alter; and to purfue, without repining, the road which Providence, who directs every thing, has marked out to us. For it is not enough to follow; and he is but a bad foldier who fighs, and marches on with reluctancy. We muft receive our orders with fpirit and cheerfulnefs, and not endeavour to flink out of the poft which is affigned us in this beautiful difpofition of things, whereof even our fufferings make a neceffary part.

Let us addrfs ourfelves to God, who governs all, as Cleanthes did in thofe admirable verfes:

Parent of nature! Mafter of the world!
Where'er thy providence directs, behold
My fteps with cheerful refignation turn.
Fate leads the willing, drags the backward on;
Why fhould I grieve, when grieving I muft bear?
Or take with guilt, what guiltlefs I might fhare?

Thus let us fpeak, and thus let us act. Refignation to the will of God is true magnanimity. But the fure mark of a pufillanimous and bafe fpirit, is to ftruggle againft, or cenfure, the difpenfations of Providence; and, inftead of mending our own conduct, to fet up for correcting that of our Maker.

.THE

INDIAN AND BRITISH OFFICER:

A TRUE STORY.

DURING the laſt war in America, a company of the Delaware Indians attacked a ſmall detachment of the Britiſh troops, and defeated them. As the Indians had greatly the advantage of ſwiftneſs of foot, and were eager in the purſuit, very few of the fugitives eſcaped ; and thoſe who fell into the enemy's hands, were treated with a cruelty of which there are not many examples even in the country.

Two of the Indians came up with a young officer, and attacked him with great fury ; as they were armed with a kind of battle-ax, which they call a tomahawk, he had no hope of eſcape, and thought only of ſelling his life as dearly as he could ; but juſt at this criſis another Indian came up, who ſeemed to be advanced in years, and was armed with a bow and arrows. The old man inſtantly drew his bow ; but after having taken his aim at the officer, he ſuddenly dropped the point of his arrow, and interpoſed between him and his purſuers, who were about to cut him in pieces—they retired with reſpect.

The old man then took the officer by the hand, ſoothed him into confidence by careſſes ; and, having conducted him to his hut, treated him with a kindneſs which did honour to his profeſſions. He made him leſs a ſlave than a *companion*, taught him the language of the country, and inſtructed him in the rude arts that are practiſed by the inhabitants. They lived together in the moſt cordial amity ; and the young officer found nothing to regret, but that ſometimes the old man fix-ed his eyes upon him, and, having regarded him for

ſome

some minutes, with a steady and silent attention, burst into tears.

In the mean time the spring returned ; and the·Indians having recourse to their arms, again took the ·field.   The old man, who was still vigorous, and well able to bear the fatigues of war, set out with them, and was accompanied by his prisoner.   They marched above two hundred leagues, across the forest, and came at length to a plain where the British forces were encamped.   The old man showed his prisoner the tents at a distance, at the same time remarked his countenance with the most diligent attention.   " There," says he, " are your countrymen ; there is the enemy who wait to give us battle.   Remember, that I have saved thy life, that I have taught thee to construct a canoe, and to arm thyself with a bow and arrows ; to surprise the beaver in the forest, to wield the tomahawk, and to scalp the enemy.   What wast thou when I first took thee to my hut ? Thy hands were those of an infant ; they were fit neither to procure thee sustenance nor safety.   Thy soul was in utter darkness : thou wast ignorant of every thing ; and thou owest all things to me.   Wilt thou then go over to thy nation, and take up the hatchet against us ?"

The officer replied, " That he would rather lose his own life than take away that of his deliverer."   The Indian then bending down his head, and covering his face with both his hands, stood some time silent : then looking earnestly at his prisoner, he said, in a voice that was at once softened by tenderness and grief, " Hast thou a father ?"—" My father," said the young man, " was alive when I left my country."— " Alas," said the Indian, " how wretched must he be !" He paused a moment, and then added, " Dost thou know that I have been a father ? I am a father no more.   I saw my son fall in battle ; he fought at my side ; I saw him expire ! but he died like a man.

He

He was covered with wounds when he fell dead at my feet ; but I have revenged him !"

He pronounced thefe words with the utmoft vehemence ; his body fhook with an univerfal tremor ; and he was almoft ftifled with fighs that he would not fuffer to efcape him. There was a keen reftleffnefs in his eye ; but no tear would flow to his relief. At length he became calm by degrees, and turning towards the eaft, where the fun was then rifing, " Doft thou fee," faid he to the young officer, " the beauty of that fky, which fparkles with prevailing day ? and haft thou pleafure in the fight ?"—" Yes," replied the young officer, " I have pleafure in the beauty of fo fine a fky."—" I have none," faid the Indian ! and his tears then found their way.

A few minutes after he fhowed the young man a magnolia in full bloom. " Doft thou fee that beautiful tree ?" fays he ; " and doft thou look upon it with pleafure ?"—" Yes," replied the officer, " I do look with pleafure upon that beautiful tree."—" I have pleafure in looking upon it no more," faid the Indian haftily ; and immediately added, " Go, return to thy countrymen, that thy father may ftill have pleafure when he fees the fun rife in the morning, and the trees bloffom in the fpring."

ON

DISSIMULATION AND SINCERITY:

A FRAGMENT.

DISSIMULATION in youth is the fore-runner of perfidy in old age. Its firft appearance is the fatal omen of growing depravity and future fhame. It degrades parts and learning, obfcures the luftre of every accomplifhment, and finks you into contempt with

E   God

God and man.   As you value, therefore, the approbation of heaven, or the efteem of the world, cultivate the love of truth.

In all your proceedings be direct and confiftent.
Sincerity and candour poffefs the moft powerful
charms ; they befpeak univerfal favour, and carry an
apology for almoft every failing.   The path of truth
is a plain and fafe path ; that of falfehood is a perplexing maze. . . . .

ON ORATORY ;

OR,

PUBLIC SPEAKING.

A FRAGMENT.

IT is certain that proper geftures and exertions of
the voice cannot be too much ftudied by a public
orator. They are a kind of comment to what he
utters ; and enforce every thing he fays, with weak
hearers, better than the ftrongeft arguments he can
make ufe of. They keep the audience awake, and
fix their attention to what is delivered to them ; at
the fame time that they fhow the fpeaker is in ear-
neft, and affected himfelf with what he fo paffionate-
ly recommends to others.

We are told, that the great Latin orator very much
impaired his health by the vehemence of action with
which he ufed to deliver himfelf. The Greek orator
was likewife fo very famous for this particular in
rhetoric, that one of his antagonifts, whom he had banifhed from Athens, reading over the oration which
had procured his banifhment, and feeing his friends
admire it, could not forbear afking them, If they
                                                    were

were fo much affected by the bare *reading* of it, how much more they would have been alarmed, had they heard him actually throwing out fuch a ftorm of elo-quence ? . . . . . · · ·

—————◦◦◦—————

THE RURAL PROSPECT:

A SOLILOQUY.

Reflective minds are pleas'd with rural fcenes.

WHAT a delightful profpect does this lofty rock afford one who admires the fimplicity and magnifi-cence of nature !

What freſhnefs in the air ! Every breeze is em-balmed ! What fragrance in the herbs ! They are fpringing around me ;. they vegetate the very rock, and cover its fummit and fides with verdure. The day-break begins to diffipate the fhades of night ; but the dawning light comes on fo gently, that the va-pours are imperceptably difpelled. The dark veil which lately hung upon the brow of the hill, is removed for a mantle perfectly. tranfparent. Already one half of the heavens is illuminated. The birth of a new morning is announced by the voice of animated nature.

The rifing zephyr ruftles among the leaves. From the neighbouring cottages afcend the wreaths of fmoke. The planet Venus, alone, difputes for a while the empire of the morning ; but, after the con-tiſt of a few minutes, fhe retires vanquifhed, and leaves the triumph of Aurora complete. And now her tri-umph is indeed rapid. Ah ! too lively an emblem of human happinefs. Nothing fo brilliant while it is advancing ; nor any thing fo fhort as its continuance.

The

The tender colours of the morn prefently give place to the more animated fire and hues of noon! The radiant foverign of day feems vertically to dart his glories into the very bowels of the earth.

Thus feated upon a jutting of the rock, I am more delighted than in viewing the beft ordered fuite of rooms in the world. Methinks I could voluntarily yield up the refidue of life, to this moral folitude.

The panting animals feek the fhade; the birds make to themfelves curtains and bowers of the verdent branches; They all pafs in repofe and covert, thofe hours when their food is robbed of its dewy frefhnefs; but the kindly drops of evening fhall reftore its relifh...

. . . .

The fun is preparing to fet; the frefhing zephyrs of the clofing day attend him; a light more foft and delicate defcends from the tops of the trees and gilds their moffy trunks. I breathe the charming odours, which come wafted to me by the balmy zephyrs. All is fweetnefs and ferenity. It feems as if Flora came to this very fpot, to braid her beautiful treffes, to bathe in the ftream that furrounds me, and expand the fragrance which enriches them. Philofophy, reafon, and innocence, are here met together: Ah; that I could forever refide on this charming rock, where every object endeavours to fix me.

Far from the bufy, crowded, lov'd refort
  Of wealth and pomp, and pleafure's frolic band,
Let me retire no greater joys I court
  Than fuch as flow from Nature's bounteous hand.

CONTEMP:

CONTEMPLATIONS by MOONLIGHT.-

Retire, the world shut out; thy thoughts call home.
NIGHT THOUGHTS.

I WAS a few evenings since indulging in a contemplation by moonlight. The beauty of the firmament, and the balminess of the air, together with the many objects which were set off with a sort of shaded silver, all conspired to fill the mind with a series of moral considerations on the immense wisdom and benevolence of the Deity, who hath in his division of time, so admirably disposed the opposite periods of light and darkness; as it would be impossible to take that repose which is requisite to the renovation of nature, while the beams of the sun and the bustle of the world obtruded; and not less inconvenient, to pursue our common business or pleasures, under the zenith of meridian obscurity.

No sooner has the day shut in, than every thing seems to invite us to share the universal pause of nature. Creation appears to feel the influence of sleep, and surrounding silence sooths the passions into a calm while lassitude prepares us for slumber. It might convince the sceptic, were he to reflect on the stupendous works of the Author of night, and of his great tenderness and vigilance over us and the weary world in this solemn scene. While the senses of man are lapt in the sweets of repose, and every head reclining on its pillow, he still guides the spheres in their motion, and regulates the planets in their annual rotations.

His dews fall silent and salutary on the verdent earth, freshen the herb, and suckle the flower, to gladden the waking morn. He extends his guardian eye over the habitable globe, and, without disturbing his creatures, conducts the moon through her circuit; and having drawn shade above shade till all is enveloped in

E 2   a mid--

a midnight gloom, he gradually withdraws the veil, and watches the progrefs of the rofy dawn. Then having unfhadowed the laft appearance of night, he delights the world with revifited light, and paints all his benevolence in the eye of the morning ; till all his bleff-ings are again prefented full and ardent by the glories: of his rifen fun.

There is not, I think, any time wherein a good man can fo happily gratify his favourite reflections as midnight ; when, confcious, warm, and infpired, he beholds the hemifphere a blaze of worlds, and confiders that his fellow-creatures are reviving their fpirits under the influence of fleep, and during that fleep, under the immediate guardianfhip of God, whofe invifible attendance he confiders as protecting every abforbed fenfe and clofed eye. His mind enlarges and dilates as it revolves thefe mercies, till, elevating itfelf to a pitch of a more fublime and lofty nature, he foars into heaven itfelf ; and becomes fo far abftracted in the mighty idea, that, grafping all that is ftupendous and amazing, he falls into a trance of aftonifhment, and lofes every faculty of fenfe in incomprehenfion; till, recovering he finds new objects demanding his veneration, and frefh inftances of eternal benevolence, rectitude, and divinity.

The night is alfo the hour of facred contemplation. The luftre of the ftars, the ftillnefs of the air, the filence of the fcene, and the awfulnefs of the feafon, all confpire to heighten our ideas, and overwhelm the heart in a flood of meditations, drawn from thofe inexhauftible fources of praife and adoration.

It is in thefe fober retirements, when we give ourfelves up to the wonders of God and nature, that we are beft able to begin the tafk of reformation, or purfue the bufinefs of unoftentatious prayer. Then no intemperate intrufions allure us, no infinuating temptations entice, nor any unruly paffions difturb or

ruffle

ruffle the bosom, which is then most easily opened to admit sincerity, contrition, penitence, and wisdom.

THE SPRING OF TRUE FELICITY

IN

EVERY PERIOD OF LIFE.

AN INTERESTING ESSAY.

The wish of all, but truly known by few.

IN respect of happiness and felicity, none evince a
greater contrariety of sentiment concerning them,
than those who are just entering into life, and those
who are about to leave it.. There are, indeed, few
things in which the opinions of youth and age agree;
and from such dissimilarity, of course, arises the general dissaffection between them.. Each, perhaps, follows
his favourite pursuit with too much eagerness. In
age, the ultimatum is *gain*, if not avarice; in youth,
it is liberality, if not *profusion*.. An old man grows
tenacious of every thing; and, when the least capable
of enjoyment, augments his wishes in proportion to the
decrease of his necessities.

He finds satisfaction in the most trifling possessions,
not because they are useful, but because they are so
much added to the heap. His organs are dim, his
appetite fanciful. Unequal to toil, and difficult of
utterance, yet he recounts with unwearied exactness
his boyish frolics, and the atchievements of
his manhood. Fond remembrance, proud recollection, and the tale of all he recollects and all he re-
members, constitute his chief pleasures; nor can we
give an higher pleasure to him whom time has made
venerable,

venerable, than by directing the converfation into a channel which may afford him opportunity to relate the wonders of his youth, and liften while he rehearfes the miracles of his life.

Youth, on the contrary, neglecting the paft, and full of ardent fpirit, preffes on to the future, animated by hope, and urged forwards by curiofity: The young man derives no confolation from what is gone before, but depends on the prefent and future. He is impatient for action. His foul is all vivacity, and his body all vigour. He pants with expectation, and begins his career with intrepidity and perfeverance. He is neither deterred by danger, nor depreffed by difappointment. Strength of conftitution, redundancy of fpirits, natural to that period of life, and a powerful defire of diftinctions, with a love of novelty, enable him to encounter difficulties, and fpurn at hazard.

To trace this contraft fomewhat farther. In a fhort time the ftripling, in the progrefs of life fees fit objects to engage and excite every paffion ; and every paffion has by turns its dominion over him, its portion of pain and pleafure, or of that mixture which tinges both. The tendernefs of *love*, being the ftrongeft, is commonly the firft impreffion. The youthful adventurer refigns his heart and its affections to beauty and to virtue ; and now his chief aim is to evince his courage, his honour, and his talents, becaufe thefe beft recommend him to the fofter fex. A pure love is the beft encourager, and not feldom the beft friend, of virtue

The thirft of public glory and applaufe now gives way to domeftic cares : A tender partner and a rifing offspring infpire the moft ferious care, and pleafure is connected with folicitude. To the vigilance and affiduity of the hufband and the parent, fucceed, gradually, the love of eafe, and a wifh to retire from

the

the obtrufions of the world. The declining man now fighs for fome retreat which may repel the attacks of farther difappointment, anxiety, and vexation. Solitude becomes in his eye as enchanting, at prefent, as fociety was before. Security from interruption, a warm fire, and an elbow-chair, prove now more agreeable to the veteran, than all the enchantments of folly, praife, and frolic ; and even the love of narration lofes its power.

Memory is now the only purveyor of his entertainment ; and to her he refers himfelf for filent remembrance of the paft. At length his views narrow to a point, and the delights of youth are totally fubverted ; and prefently, he who in the morning of exiftence delighted chiefly in the happinefs of others, will, in the gloom of its night, find a ftronger propenfity to afford comfort only to himfelf ; and when the fun of human life is fet, the awful hour will approach, when the paffing-bell fhall feelingly declare, that the veteran has finifhed his earthly courfe, and the places that lately knew him, know him no more.

Happinefs is a plant of celeftial extraction, fet by the hand of God in the centre of this world, which branches thence by millions of ramifications over every part of it. Its bloffom and fruit may be, and are in a degree, enjoyed by every one who has either the fkill, the difcretion, or the induftry, to cultivate it. In fhort, it grows by nature in every mind, and will flourifh long therein, if not choaked by the weeds of impiety, folly, and perverfenefs.

Human happinefs confifts in the filent, facred applaufe of a good confcience, and, however varioufly it is purfued, is attainable only by the practice of virtue, a decency of manners, and dignity of conduct.

From the moment the eye opens on the light, to that in which death draws over its vifion an eternal curtain, our main, and indeed only end, is felicity.

ty. To be happy, every paſſion, ſenſe, perception, and faculty, every corporeal and moral power, is rouſed to its higheſt pitch of activity and exertion. Yet it is amazing to remark, how the ſame beings, in the ſame purſuit, ſhould vary in their chaſe.

Every man has in object of bliſs congenial to his diſpoſition ; an enjoyment characteriſtic of his mind and which is ſeldom or never the favourite pleaſure of any other.

Happineſs, like wit, may be divided into two parts ; that which is *real*, and that which is *fantaſtical*, : or, like gold, into the ſterling and the baſe. Much of what the world honours with the appellation of Felicity, is the chimera of an heated imagination ; and ſtill more is the painting of popular folly. Under theſe heads we may arrange the pride of anceſtry, the farce of ſplendour, the bubble of applauſe, the waſte of magnificence, the apparatus of ſtation, and the inſolence of birth. Theſe proceed from a miſtake in the means, and are diſappointed of the end.

Mankind would be leſs unhappy, would they conſtantly remember, that they are only beings of a world which like themſelves, is in continual decay ; and that every ſtate muſt inevitably feel more or leſs the tax levied on it by frail mortality.

EMILIUS AND CLARA ;
OR,
THE HAPPY PAIR.

Each was to each a dearer ſelf.   THOMSON.

EVERY day, after work Emilius congratulated himſelf upon the hours of relaxation, which permitted him to rejoin Clara, in whom he felt, at every return,

turn, new attractions. Seated at her fide over their frugal blaze, under the thatch of their little cottage, and balancing upon his knees one of his infants, while the other hung harmlefsly at the breaft of its mother, he forgot his fatigues; he forgot that he had been labouring ever fince the fun got up, even to his going down : or, even if he did remember his wearinefs, the recollection of exertions by which he fed his babes, faw them innocently eating the bread he had earned, and merited a tender fmile from his Clara, rendered the whole more touching. Tranfported by thefe moft agreeable profpects, nothing difturbed their repofe : "All was truly full." The hufband, the wife, and their children, were together. Their imaginations could picture nothing fofter, nothing happier than themfelves.

The fight of their children always augmented their felicity. They were not lefs touched with an embarrafsment they perceived in thefe little creatures, while they were ftammering to exprefs their tendernefs, and while their pains were rewarded by a thoufand cares and careffes. What a fource of pleafure was it to Emilius and Clara, to interpret their wills ! to fatisfy their defires, and to condefcend even to join in their innocent paftimes !

Ah ! how happy was Emilius, when he felt the tender hands of his children ftruggling to embrace his own, hardened as they were by work, and embrowned by the wind and weather! The fon, one day, was curious to know the reafon of this : "And why, papa (faid he), is not your hand as foft as mine ? Why is it fo hard, papa ?"—" In making bread for you and your mother," replied Emilius, with paternal and gentle dignity. " It is, you fee, almoft worn out in the fervice."—" Oh, oh ! (cried the child,) is that the cafe ?' Well, then, by the time it has made us a little more bread, mine will grow ftout enough to make bread

too ;

too ; and then we fhall fee, papa, whofe will be hardeft." The child copied the virtuous pride of the
father : Emilius blufhed with joy, and Clara fhed a
tear.

EXTRAVAGANCE AND GENEROSITY CONTRASTED.

Spare to fpend, and fpend to fpare.

EXTRAVAGANCE is not lefs deftructive of a
man's happinefs than avarice ; and if it be lefs hateful to the world in general, it is more pernicious to
private families and intimate connexions. It keeps
a man always needy, always in want ; it goes beyond this, and compels the naturally generous and
honeft heart to be guilty of the meaneft peculation.
Thus extravegance and flafhes of generofity, are not
at all incompatible qualities in the fame breaft with
the moft rapacious avarice. Indeed I never knew a
prodigal who was not in fome inftances guilty of
meannefs. If you would look for the *true* generofity, you will probably find it among thofe, who let
not vanity or the love of pleafure keep them in perpetual neceffity.

However paradoxical it might feem, if we fhould
fay that a man with forty pounds a year is rich, and
at the fame time call one with twice as many thoufands poor, yet this is certainly very often the cafe ;
for whatever a man's income be, if he is fatisfied
therewith, and can limit his expenfes within its
bounds, he is undoubtedly in happy circumftances.
While he who avaricioufly pines for more, or whofe
extravagant expenfes ftretch beyond what he has
means to fupply, however great his eftate, is ever in
poverty, or may juftly fear it.

Whatever

Whatever they may poffefs, people, in reality, with regard to pecuniary circumftances, may be divided into *three* claffes ; thofe in a thriving condition, whofe annual income yields a faving beyond their ufual expenfe ; thofe who, perhaps with fome difficulty, keep upon a balance ; and thofe who run into greater expenfe than they have means to fupport, without a decay of fortune.

REFLECTIONS

ON

AMUSEMENTS AND DIVERSIONS.

Amufement's the word.

THE human mind naturally fhudders at the idea of diffolution, and would be unable to fupport itfelf under this gloomy reflection, did not the profpect of a future ftate of happinefs, beget that fortitude which enables us to entertain the thought with magnanimity. The foul triumphs in the belief of a glorious immortality ; and looks down upon this prefent tranfient life, as the veftibule to a more permanent and durable exiftence. If then we have a better and more folid foundation for our expectations than what mortality affords us, the prefent enjoyments of life will be lefs regarded, than the more fubftantial ones to be inherited in the world to come.

An attentive furvey of the nature of man will difcover an eager propenfity in him to pleafure, diverfion, and novelty ; he is delighted with a variety of amufements, and a diverfity of fcenes. Hence the many different places of entertainment, devoted to the gratification of this fluctuating defire.

The human frame is compofed of different ingredients, intermixed with the folid and the gay, the ferious and the trifling ; and therefore to apply ourfelves

F

ſelves too cloſely to the obſervation of ſerious objects, without relaxing our minds on neceſſary occaſions from buſineſs and ſtudy, would be attended with great prejudice. For as too much labour diſorders and enervates the whole frame, ſo too intenſe an application of the mind to ſtudious exerciſes, weakens its native energy, and creates a kind of ſtupefaction in our intellectual ſtructure.

It is reported of the great Ageſilaus, that he frequently amuſed himſelf with his children, by joining in their puerile ſports : Nor was he aſhamed, when ſurpriſed riding on a ſtick round his own hall. Very different is the man whoſe days are ſpent in continual ſolitude, who is perpetually employed in ſtudious reſearches, and in indulging the moſt gloomy and melancholy reflections ; he looks down with a ſupercilious air on all preſent recreations and enjoyments, and judging of other men's actions from his own pedantic and narrow notions, condemns them as the reſult of the utmoſt folly and ſtupidity.

How miſerable is the condition of ſuch a mortal ! The moſt ſuperficial examination will convince us of the anguiſh and uneaſineſs in which he is continually involved, who by his indiſcreet behaviour embitters the very ſweets of life ; and renders that a curſe, which by a proper uſe and improvement might be a real bleſſing.

ON THE BENEFITS OF EXERCISE.

Exerciſe increaſeth ſtrength.

AS man is a compound of ſoul and body, he is under an obligation of a double ſcheme of duty ; and as labour and exerciſe conduce to the health of the body, ſo do ſtudy and contemplation to that of the mind for ſtudy ſtrengthens the mind, as exercife

cife does the body. The labour of the body frees us from the pains of the mind, and this it is which makes the poor happy. The mind, like the body, grows tired by being too long in one pofture. The end of diverfion is to unbend the foul, deceive the cares, fweeten the toils, and fmooth the ruggednefs of life.

As the body is maintained by repletion and eva-cuation, fo is the mind by employment and relaxation. Difficulty ftrengthens the mind, as labour does the body. Life and happinefs confift in action and em-ployment. Active and mafculine fpirits, in the vi-gour of youth, neither can, or ought to be at reft. If they debar themfelves from a nobler object, their defires will move downwards, and they will feel themfelves actuated by fome low and abject paffion or purfuit. As the fweeteft rofe grows upon the fharpeft prickles, fo the hardeft labour brings forth the fweeteft profits. The end of labour is reft ; what brightnefs is to ruft, labour is to idlenefs ; idlenefs is the ruft of the mind, and the inlet to all misfortunes. Diligence is the mother of Virtue.

When it is known, fays Plato, how exercife pro-duces digeftion, and promotes health, comlinefs, and ftrength, there will be no occafion to enjoin the ufe of fuch exercife by a law ; or to enforce an attention to it on the candidates for health, vigour and perfonal charms.

THE WISDOM OF PROVIDENCE

IN THE

VARIETY OF THE SEASONS.

WRITTEN IN THE SPRING.

IN contemplating on the various fcenes of life, the viciffitudes of the feafons, the perfect regularity, order, and harmony of nature, we cannot but be filled with
wonder

wonder and admiration, at the consummate wisdom, and beneficence of the all-wise and gracious Creator. His consummate wisdom, and goodness have made the various seasons of the year, perfectly consonant to the refined feelings of man, and peculiarly adapted them to the universal preservation of nature. Dreary winter is past ; its severe cold is mitigated ; the returning zephyrs dissolve the fleecy snow, unlock the frozen streams, which overflow the extensive meadows, and enrich the teeming earth.

At length, the rapid streams begin to glide gently within their banks ; the spacious meadows soon receive their usual verdure, and the whole face of nature assumes a cheerful aspect. By the refreshing showers and vivifying power of the genial sun, we behold the rapid and amazing progress of vegetation.

What is more pleasing to the eye, or grateful to the imagination, than the agreeable and delightsome return of spring ? The beauties of nature at once expel the gloomy cares of dreary winter. The benign influences of the sun give a brisk circulation to the animal fluids, and happily tend to promote the propagation of animated nature. In the spring we behold the buds putting forth their blossoms ; in summer we meet with the charming prospect of enamelled fields, which promise a rich profusion of autumnal fruits.

These delightful scenes afford to man a pleasing anticipation of enjoying the bounties of providence, cheer him in adversity, and support him under the various misfortunes incident to human life. In the spring, when we behold plants and flowers peeping out of the ground, reviving, and flourishing at the approach of the vernal sun—when we behold the seed, which the laborious husbandman casts into the earth, starting into life, and rising into beauty, from the remainder of that which perished in the preceding autumn, tamn, we are filled with the moſt pleaſing ſenſations of the univerſal revivefcence of Nature.

The warm and invigorating fun produces myriads of infects, which have been lifelefs through the hoary froſts of winter. The herds now go forth to graze on the verdant plains. The innumerable flocks quit their folds, with their young, to feed on the diftant mountains. The matin lark, with all the charming choir, whom kind Nature wakes to cheerfulnefs and love, tune their melodious voices to hail the welcome returning ſpring. The buſy bee flies over the fields, and extracts the liquid ſweets from every flower. How pleaſing! how wonderful! are the ſcenes preſented to our view!

The ſpring of the year ſeems ſtrikingly emblematical of that grand and univerſal reſurrection, which ſhall commenſe at the final confummation of all things; may its beauties therefore raiſe our affections to thoſe ſuperior regions of bliſs, into which the truly virtuous ſhall then enter, and for ever enjoy an unfading and eternal ſpring.

-----◦◦◦◦-----

THE FOLLY OF AVARICE.

Man wants but little, nor that little long. Dr. YOUNG.

IT is generally found, that he who inherits the fortune of a miſer, has the paſſions of a prodigal; and if one man collects as a reſervoir, his fucceſſor plays off as a fountain. By which means, what was before hoarded up carefully, now takes unto inſelf wings, and flies away; and as a ſquanderer is pretty expeditious in his expenſes, that haſte makes up for the loſt time, and brings the balance of public good once more upon the equilibrium.

F 2.   Notwithſtanding

Notwithftanding thefe obfervations, we muft allow
neither to the fpendthrift nor mifer more merit than
is their due.   Out of much evil we may extract fome
good ; as honey may be extracted from poifons ; and
this is the light in which thefe perfons muft be view-
ed.   Let us forbear to enroll them, on the lift of
fame, amongft the more honourable or valuable orders of men.

'The prince who ardently ftudies the welfare, the
happinefs, and felicity of his people ; the father
who trains his family to piety and virtue ; the man
of fcience who thinks and writes for the improvement
of the human heart, and embellifhment of the human underftanding ; the merchant who increafes our
wealth, and advances our pleafure ; the artificer who
prefents us with an elegant and ufeful invention ; the
private gentlemen who diffufes comfort through his
neighbourhood ; and the woman whofe examples extends the influence of goodnefs, whofe integrity infpires
confidence, and whofe beauty animates to tendernefs,
are all refpectable characters, and deferve univerfal regard.

ON THE EDUCATION OF YOUTH.

AN ESSAY.

'Tis education forms the youthful mind,
For as the bough is bent the tree's inclin'd.

IT has been the comparifon of a celebrated author,
that as marble taken out of the quarry fhows none of
its inherent beauties, till it has undergone the labour
of the polifher ; fo education, when it works upon an
ingenuous mind, brings out to view every latent
perfection, which without fuch helps are never able to
make

make their appearance. And let me add to this observation, that if we take the trouble to look around us we shall find very few, to whom Nature has been such a niggard of her gifts, that they are not capable of shining in *one* sphere of science or another. Since then there is a certain bias towards knowledge, in almost every mind, which may be strengthened and improved by proper care ; I think parents should consider, in the neglect of so essential a point, they do not commit a *private* injury only, as thereby they starve posterity, and defraud our country, of those persons who, under better management, might perhaps make an eminent figure in the world.

Indeed, that the difference to be perceived in the manners and abilities of men proceeds more from education, than from any imperfections or advantages derived from their original formation, is a matter so long agreed on by philosophers, that to advance any thing in favour of it in this place appears altogether unnecessary. I cannot help recollecting a story, related by Plutarch, of Lycurgus, the Spartan lawgiver, which will serve to set the matter in a yet stronger light.

He took two whelps of the same litter, and ordered them to be bred in a quite different manner ; a while after he took an occasion, in an assembly of the people, to discourse of what great advantage the customary practice of wholesome instructions and precepts was to the attainment of virtue ; in the close of this harrangue, he told them, he would make an appeal to their senses, and let them see a demonstration of his words, by example. Upon this, the two whelps were ordered to be brought into the hall, and there was set down to them a dish of fragments, and a live hare. One of the dogs (as he had been bred) flies upon the hare, and the other as greedily runs to the fragments.

While

While the people were mufing to find out the moral of this odd proceeding ; " This," fays Lycurgus,
" is purfuant to what I before told you ; for, fee,
thefe whelps do as they were bred, and though they
were both of the fame litter, yet the diverfity of
breeding hath made the one a good hound, and
the other a cur, good for nothing, but to lick pots or
difhes."

Let me add to this obfervation, and example, that
youth is the proper and only feafon for education ;
for if it be neglected then, it will be in vain to think
of remedying the overfight in more advanced years*;
it will be too late to think of fowing it, when maturity has rendered the mind ftubborn and inflexible ; and
when, inftead of receiving the feeds, it fhould be bringing forth the fruits of inftruction.

But there is one point in the article of education,
which is more effential than any of the reft ; I mean
the great care that ought to be taken to form youth
to the principles of religion.   Vice, if we may believe the general complaint, grows fo malignant now-
a-days, that it is almoft impoffible to keep young people from the fpreading contagion, if we venture them
abroad, and truft to chance or inclination, for the
choice of their company : it is therefore the reward
of virtue‡; and a perfect fenfe of their duty to God†,
which are the great and valuable things to be taught
them.   All other confiderations and accomplifhments
fhould give way to thefe ; thefe are the folid and fubftantial good we fhould labour to implant and faften
in their tender minds, neither fhould we ceafe our endeavours

---

* Youth is the time to learn from, and age to teach by,
precept and *example.*
‡ Virtue is its own reward.
† The fear of the Lord is the beginning of wifdom.

deavours fo to do till they have attained a true relifh
of them, and placed their ftrength, their glory, and
their pleafure in them.

Knowledge of the world is certainly of great im-
portance to young people, and methods fhould be taken to give them an infight into the manners of mankind; left, when they come to play their feveral parts
amongft them, they fhould be at a lofs how to act, and
make a thoufand blunders, which experience alone
can put a ftop to.   But here I fhall be told, that *experience* fhould be the grand inftructor, it being impoffible to acquire a perfect knowledge of the world by
any other means than by a diffufive commerce with
mankind.

The obfervation is certainly juft ; however, though
precept cannot in this cafe abfolutely fupply the place
of example ‡, it may be a very ufeful and requifite pre-
parative : as ftudying the *map* of a country, is of great
affiftance to us when we come to make a journey
through it.

———◇◇◇———

REFLECTIONS

ON THE

VALUE OF TIME.

Time wafted is *exiftence*, us'd is *life*   DR. YOUNG.

———

THERE is nothing in this life which we ought to
fet a greater value upon than time, and it becomes
every one fo to ufe, as to improve it.   Many are defirous of putting off repentance to a future time, yet
if they would but recollect how fleet the minutes are,
                                              they

———
‡ Good examples corroborate and eftablifh good precepts.

they never would be fo eager to defer it even another day; for fo uncertain is the life of man, that he, who is to-day in perfect health, may, to-morrow, be oppreffed with ficknefs, and in a few days, be conveyed to the filent grave.

Every young man fhould appropriate a portion of the day to his ftudies, and, at the fame time, diveft himfelf of every thought which is liable to diftract his attention : for unlefs we do in our youth make a proper ufe of that time which we ought to dedicate to the improvement of our minds, we fhall find, when we go out into the world, that we have laboured under fad defects and difadvantages. But if we are defirous to imitate the excellent examples which Newton, Homer, Demofthenes, and other great men afford us, we muft apply ourfelves to our ftudies with a fixt attention, fince it is that alone which will enable us to arrive at the fummit of knowledge.

Had either of thefe been diftracted with trifling thoughts, the rays of genius thus diverging from their proper focus, had loft their efficacy, and procured little or no fame to names now fo celebrated. The ftories of Melancthon and Titus Vefpafian, afford ftriking lectures on the value of time, the one of which was, that whenever he made an appointment, he expected not only the hour, but the *minutes* to be fixed, that the day might not run out in the idlenefs of fufpence. The other was, if at any time a day had elapfed, in which he had done no good, he would exclaim, " My friends, I have loft a day."

As time, like money, may be loft by unfeafonable profufion, it is the duty of every one to endeavour to imitate the example of thefe great men, that we all may properly efteem its value, and lament the lofs of it, as a mifer would that of his riches. The ftage of life might be made a perpetual fountain of agreeable and ufeful entertainments, were we to regulate

gulate it by a proper diftribution of our time. There is nothing which unbends the mind more agreeably than the converfation of a well-chofen friend. It eafes and unloads it, clears and improves the underftanding, produces in us ufeful thoughts and knowledge ; and, in a word, finds employment for moft of the vacant hours of life.

A gentleman that has a tafte for *mufic, drawing, or painting,* acts wifely if he allots a portion of his time to one of thofe pleafing arts. The cultivation of plants and flowers, an agreeable amufement in a *country* life, may alfo be found ufeful, to thofe who are poffeffed of *that* tafte. But of all the rational amufements of life, there is none more proper to fill up its vacant fpaces, than *reading* fome ufeful and entertaining authors*. Since, then, time cannot be recalled, it becomes every one to be folicitous for the improvement of every part of it ; and let us not hoard up a *fhilling* with care, whilft that which is above the price of the greateft eftate paffes by unnoticed, and confequently unimproved.

There is a remarkable inftance of parfimony of time in one of Pliny's Letters, where he gives an account of the various methods he ufed to fill up every vacancy : after feveral employments which he enumerates, fometimes, fays he, I hunt ; but even then I carry with me a pocket-book, that whilft my fervants are bufied in difpofing of the nets, I may be employed in fomething that may be ufeful to me in my ftudies ; and that if I mifs of my game, I may at leaft bring home fome cf my own thoughts with me, and not have the mortification of having caught nothing all day.

* A friend, a book, the ftealing hours fecure,

And mark them down for wifdom. THOMSON.

THE

THE LAST DYING WORDS OF AN OFFICER IN THE ARMY.

Courage in Death.

ALL-bountiful Heaven! to whofe protecting arm I owe my life in the imminent dangers of battle; and to whom I am indebted for the numerous bleffings of it, amidft the menaces of avowed enemies, and the fecret fappings of perfidious friends.—Thine too are the domeftic joys which I have participated with the beft of wives, now, alas! no more.—Juft Heaven, why am I now torn from the two dear pledges of our mutual loves, my beloved daughters, at the very moment too, when I feemed to poffefs the means of providing for them, in a manner adequate to a parent's fondeft wifhes?

The ways of Heaven are often myfterious, but are always juft and righteous; no doubts of its goodnefs can poffibly cloud my departing moments.—Oh, fave my children from all the evils to which innocence, beauty, and virtue, efpecially if they wear a *female* form, are expofed.—To my country too I intruft my beloved girls: for I have ferved my country when it needed my help. But, oh! my children! had I not the firmeft affurance, that Heaven, and all good men, would be your friends, I fhould feel pangs worfe than the agonies of death which now come faft upon me, to leave you thus unprotected and unprovided, to conflict with a wicked and feducing world.

But the greateft of Beings is the beft of beings, and however fevere the fufferings of the good and virtuous may be, affure yourfelves of this, that a fteady adherence in the path of virtuous rectitude will meet an ample reward.—

Though I have frequently met death in the field, he is too ftrong for me now.—Oh—oh—oh—".

———

REFLECTIONS

REFLECTIONS ON REPENTANCE

IN THE

VIEWS OF DEATH.

Better late than never.

WHOEVER is advancing toward the end of life, and throws his thoughts back to what he has feen, if not *experienced*, in his progrefs through it, will be convinced he leaves more evil than good behind him ; and that even the good belonging to this life is fo mixed with evil, that however it might beguile the *firft* choice, it will hardly raife a wifh for the repetition of it. When we refleft on our helplefs painful ftate of infancy—the dangers and vices of our youth—the cares and anxieties of manhood—and the calamities of old age—who can, confiftently, lament, that he is finifhing a courfe, which, was it in his power, he feels no inclination to repeat ?

Colleft and weigh the enjoyments and the fufferings of life againft each other, and ere the balance turns, recollect the very fhort fpace of time in which they are all tranfafted—how fhort and unremembered is our infancy—how youth has flipped by us whilft we were laughing—how manhood's work engages our attention, till old age furprifes us unawares : —then fhift the experiment, and weigh this fpeck of time againft *eternity*—an eternity which God hath promifed, and which it is in our own power, affifted by divine grace, to make an happy one.

Were there nothing beyond the grave—yet, after three or four fcore years fatigue in life, we might be well contented to lie down and reft ; but when Chrift has made the grave the gate of heaven, there is no part of our progrefs, in which reafon and religion would not encourage us to exchange this life

G   for

for a better—did not earthly appetite make us relish this, and a sinful conscience make us afraid of exchanging it for a worse.

The certainty of death is a reason why we should prepare ourselves to meet it.—The truest wisdom consists in making provision for futurity, and the capacity of doing this, is what principally distinguishes man from the inferior parts of the creation.

Death does not put a period to our life ; but, as it shuts this state upon us, so it opens another, into which we must make our entrance*. This heightens the lesson of making preparation for such a change. Was death to put a period to our being, interest might direct us to make the most of this life ; but, as it is not merely the conclusion of this state, but the beginning of another, the same interest will direct us not to confine our reflections within a limit so much narrower than our being, but to make provision for a state to which we are assured we shall be called.

To be lost in dust, and for ever shut up in the chambers of the grave, had been a heavy reflection to that active principle within us, which by all its operations shows the divinity of its original, and that it is not so much a part, as a prisoner of the body. But when we consider, that death ere long shall set it at liberty, and that as soon as it has broke from its prison, it shall wing its way to those happy regions for which it was intended—this makes us bear our present state with patience, and expect the last moments of this life, as the first moments of our happiness.

The conditions on which we are to recover the happiness of the next state, are such as may make

every

---

* Mors janua vitæ.

every real Chriſtian eaſy in his expectations of it.
They are not conditions of an abſolute, *unblemiſhed*
obedience, but an obedience where true repentance
has covered the ſtains which careleſs folly may have
made. Let us but ſearch our hearts with impartial-
ity—the beſt among us will find repentance neceſſary,
and who can ſay the worſt will find it uſeleſs? Chriſt
has declared the purpoſe of his mercy, to accept re-
pentant ſinners ; nor can we preſume to ſet bounds
to that mercy, and ſay, " hitherto it ſhall go, and
no farther."

That men may be hardened in ſin beyond the power of repenting, is but too true : but that there is
a time, on this ſide the grave, when ſincere repentance ſhall find no mercy is more than we have a
right to ſay. The repentance of any ſinner, Chriſt
ſees, and Chriſt will judge ; and if he ſees it attended
with that ſincerity which he has required, it is al-
lowable to hope he will accept it. There are many
inſtances of repentance where God only knows whether it be *ſincere ;* in ſuch inſtances, we cannot pronounce poſitively that it will take place becauſe we
cannot know whether it be ſincere ; but for the very
ſame reaſon we ought not to pronounce that it will
have no effect. Take an unhappy ſinner upon his
death-bed, with all the outward expreſſions of repentance about him—what ſhall we ſay ? Shall we tell
him his repentance will be of no ſervice to him, and
ſo add to his anguiſh, as well as diſcourage him from
performing a neceſſary duty ? No ; leave this to God,
who ſearches the heart of man, and may often ſee
the ſincerity of repentance when *we* cannot ; and
where there is ſincerity there will be mercy.

CONTENT.

CONTENTMENT IN PROSPERITY.

AN ESSAY.

O be content where heaven can give no more.

NIGHT THOGHTS.

THERE are very few queftions which have more puzzled philofophers, than one in particular relating to the regimen of ourfelves in profperity and adverfity. The conteft was never finally determined, whether it was the greater bravery to moderate ourfelves in plenty, or to bear up with conftancy under the preffures of want. The difpute, I think, is not very material ; but the neceffity of contentment appears manifeftly from both fides, in order to enjoy any felicity in either condition.

Murmuring and complaint generally proceed from the difference of men's fituations in life. The fordid are apprehenfive they fhall never have enough ; and the profufe want more to animate their extravagance. They who have but fmall fortunes cannot relifh the fcantinefs of moderation ; grandeur and gaiety do not always fit eafy on the wealthy ; and the neceffitous are diffatisfied that they are expofed to the feverity of indigence.

A ftrange variety of paffions thus daily diftract the human mind, and for want of knowing how to be eafy, too many make themfelves miferable. But all thefe repinings are in reality criminal : man is properly his own tormentor ; he difquiets himfelf in vain, and by neglecting the obfervation of one eafy virtue, he never taftes the fruit of genuine contentment.—To regulate our defires, and limit our pleafures, is what I mean by contentment in a plentiful

tiful condition—a ftate which requires great circum-fpection to keep the paflions from running into excefs!

Profperity is a trying and dangerous ftate, in which, as we exercife our judgment, we fhall difplay either the greateft folly, or the moft exemplary wifdom. Good fortune is apt to delude us with its fmiles, and ftrangle us in its embraces. It unbends the mind, and flackens the powers of it ; and, by a fraudulent gratification of fenfe, it infenfibly fteals away the ufe of our reafon. Many have ftood inflexible under the fhock of poverty, who have afterwards fallen a facri-fice to a plentiful fortune.

Temptations to a fatal fecurity are too preva-lent, when the mind is lulled into carelefsnefs and neglect. We apprehend no difficulty, becaufe we feel none ; and we promife ourfelves fafety, becaufe a treacherous confidence blinds us to our danger.

But when fortune fmiles, let us roufe up our circumfpection. Our paflions then require a tight rein, left our actions fhould hurry us into in-folence and prefumption. Confidence in our pofref-fions is too apt to obliterate the remembrance of duty, and too great an opinion of our own merit, fometimes creates a forgetfulnefs of our dependance on God.

The defires, it is plain, have a tendency to violence ; and an eafy affluence, inftead of fatisfying, pufhes them on to further gratifications. When the heart is thus enlarged, and the fpirits too volatile, we are naturally inclined to embark in new undertakings : we are infenfible of any difficulties which fhould ftop us in our career, and, for want of proper reftraint, our defires hurry us into extravagance, which feldom ends in any thing but ruin.

Thus fallen from the fummit of grandeur, we fhall become the objects of fcorn and contempt.

G 2   Whilft

Whilst our fields stood thick with corn, and our garners abounded with all manners of stores, the sycophants were ready to attend our tables, din our ears with compliment, and try to persuade us that we were more than men: but no sooner is the scene changed, and a sad alteration appears in our circumstances, than these infamous animals all vanish, and (like vermin which fly from a tottering house) forsake and abandon us in our misfortunes.

The virtue of contentment, in the midst of prosperity, seems in this point very necessary, as it tends to preserve a good fortune in hand, and to prevent a shame which must be grating on the loss of it. A strict vigilance would keep passion within due bounds. Our fall from an elevated station might be prevented by an evenness of temper, and a proper circumspection; but for want of it our misfortune will be reflected on with remorse, and the invidious will rejoice, and persecute us with severity. In short, let us embrace contentment, as a most amiable virtue, and restrain our passions, as most conducive to our temporal as well as eternal welfare. Then we shall relish our enjoyments without surfeiting, and have a true taste of the delights of life, without neglecting the duties of christianity.

THE REFORMED RAKE*.

A STORY FOUNDED ON FACTS.

LORD AIMWELL was born with a great share of good sense, which he improved by an application to study; and being possessed of a very happy constitution

* That a reformed rake may make a good husband, the following story proves beyond denial; but ladies should not easily be persuaded to make trial of it, as it doubtless is very hazardous.

conftitution and an agreeable perfon, he was likely
to make a very capital figure in the world.. After he
had been fome time at the univerfity, his father fent
him with a private tutor to make the tour of Europe,
in order to enlarge his ideas, and furmount thofe pre-
judices which we are too apt to entertain againft
foreigners. His tutor was a young clergyman of a
lively imagination and ftrong paffions ; but who had
hypocrify fufficient to prevent his friends and relations difcovering his foibles. But when he was no.
longer within the compafs of their obfervation, he
gave a loofe to all his extravagances ; and finding in
his pupil a difpofition not diffimilar to his own, they
were fworn friends, and conftant companions.

At Paris, they made acquaintance with the moft.
celebrated *filles de joye*, and opera-girls ; affifted at
every fpectacle where mirth and feftivity reigned,.
and paffed a winter in one conftant courfe of liber-
tinifm and diffipation.. Lord Aimwell was detected
with the miftrefs of a captain of dragoons, who called him to account, when the French officer was run
through the fword arm. Upon this occafion, his Lordfhip's tutor was his fecond, who behaved with as
much gallantry as if he had been bred to the fword.
Hence they departed for Italy, and were at Venice
during the carnival.

Here they entered into all the fpirit of Italian luxury and refinement ; every attainable flower in the
garden of love was culled and enjoyed, till at length
a more than charming *bouquet* ingroffed all his Lordfhip's attention. He had juft framed a connexion
with Signora Calemetti, when he received the news
of the death of his father ; and his affairs calling him
immediately home, this lady agreed to accompany
him in his journey.

Upon his Lordfhip's arrival in England, he appointed his late tutor his chaplain, regulated all other
family

family bufinefs very fpeedily, and confined all his
fondeft wifhes to Signora Calemetti.. Her reign was,
however, but of a fhort date ; another miftrefs and
another fucceeded ; and finding herfelf flighted, the
quitted his houfe, and tcok refuge under the wing of
a certain rich Welch Baronet..

. His Lordfhip purfued this courfe of licentiouf-
nefs for upwards of two years, during which time he
was hurried from reflection, and immerfed in debauchery ; till at laft he met, in a private party, the
beautiful, the amiable, the accomplifhed Mifs L——s.
Struck with her uncommon charms, he found the
force of her perfections all at once affail him ; deprived of the power of utterance, he could not even
hint to her what he felt—he left the company, and
having returned home, acquainted his Chaplain with
his fituation.

The Prieft endeavoured at firft to rally his paffion ;
but finding it too deeply rooted to be diverted by
pleafantry, he undertook to be his Lordfhip's advocate.
He accordingly found means to obtain an audience
of the lady, when he intimated to her the ftate of his
Lordfhip's mind, the violence of his paffion for her,
and his ftrong defire of prefenting her with his hand.
To this fhe replied with great ferenity of temper,
" I am not a ftranger to Lord Aimwell's merit, nor
am I infenfible of the honour he propofes me ; but
I am too well acquainted with his Lordfhip's irreg-
ularities to promife myfelf the fmalleft fhare of happinefs from fuch an union." All remonftrance was
vain, fhe ftill perfifted in thefe fentiments.

When his Lordfhip was informed of her anfwer,
he was almoft diftracted, and would probably have
committed fome violence upon his perfon, had he not
been carefully watched. He now faw his paft errors
in their ftrongeft light—All his follies, all his vices,
                                        crowded

crowded upon his remembrance, and made him almost diftracted.

After recovering himfelf from the violent agitation his fpirits had been thrown into, he refolved never to recur to his former abandoned courfes; and if by his penitence and the fincerity of his reformation, he could not obtain her heart, at leaft to facrifice *his* entirely to her. He frequented every public and private place, where he judged there was a poffibility of meeting with Mifs L——s; and from fome hints fhe accidentally dropt, he found he was not abfolutely indifferent to her.

After fome months conftant attendance upon her, he refolved on a ftratagem to extort from her the acknowledgement of a mutual paffion. He had kept houfe for fome days, and it was given out he was very ill. His Lordfhip's friend, who communicated this intelligence to Mifs L——s, could perceive a very vifible alteration in her countenance upon receiving the information which convinced his Lordfhip of the probability of his fcheme. This gentleman was at a party of quadrille, where this lady affifted, when news was brought that his Lordfhip was given over, and that he intreated a vifit from her in his laft moments. At this intelligence Mifs L——s fainted. When fhe recovered, the gentleman informed her there was but one way to fave his Lordfhip's life, as fhe was his diforder, and fhe might be his cure. She confented to wait upon his Lordfhip with the gentleman; when her forrow was fo explicit, and her paffion fo amply avowed, that his Lordfhip foon recovered, and their nuptials were celebrated in a few days.

He has fince confeffed the artifice he played upon her, as his diforder was totally *imaginary*. She has forgiven him, and acknowledged fhe even approved of his plan, as it was the only means by which fhe could.

could have been tempted to have difcovered her regard for him; and had it not taken place, fhe fhould
have been deprived of the beft of hufbands, and the
moft amiable of men.

A WELL KNOWN EPITAPH

ILLUSTRATED AND IMPROVED.

Remember man, now paffing by,
As thou art now, fo once was I;
As I am now, fo muft thou be,
Prepare therefore to follow me.

WHOEVER this lover of fimplicity and truth
was, he certainly ftole the idea from the Latin motto, *Sum, Es, Fui.*

Reft happy fhade, who in thy pilgrimage through
this vale of fin and forrow, compiled this fhort but
pithy leffon for wandering travellers yet to come ;
who haft thus kindly left a memento for future ages
in words plain and fimple, yet ftrong and nervous ;
on a fubject daily feen, but hourly forgot : while
by thy direction every grinning fcalp thus befpeaks
the bufy paffenger,

" *As I am now, fo muft thou be.*"

Let us now proceed to confider the above epitaph, together with the motto, in fuch a manner, as
may conduce to general profit ; notwithftanding the
frailty of the human heart, or the folly of the author's
head.

Suth,

Sum, Es, Fui.

Remember man, now paffing by,
As thou art now, fo once was I.

Here comes in the *Ei*; and the motto and the epitaph both join in this important queftion, What art thou? Art thou the child of health, a lover of mirth, and the favorite of fun? So once was I. Does the glance of love, the flufh of fury, or the ferene look of complaifance, fparkle in thine eyes? So once they did in mine.

Active appear thy limbs, ftrong feems thy conftitution; fo once feemed mine. Art thou the child of calamity? Do difappointments thwart thy beft defigns? does affliction mar thy comfort, or loffes unexpected fpoil thy hopes? Juft fo it was with me, till death releafed my weary foul, and bowed my head in duft. Thus fpeaks that faithful monitor—*a dead man's fkull.* . . . . . .

" Wait the great teacher Death." NIGHT THOUGHTS.

REFLECTIONS

ON

THE DARLING PASSIONS

OF

MANKIND IN GENERAL.

Follies, if uncontroll'd, of ev'ry kind,
Grow into paffion, and fubdue the mind;
With fenfe and reafon hold fuperier ftrife,
And conquer honour, nature, fame, and life. MOORE.

AS

AS every man was intended to form some link in the great chain of social life, where order and convenience are supported by variety, hence are they by nature endowed not only with different tallents and capacities, but with as different tempers and inclinations. And it is as these are duly regulated by reason, prudence, justice, and virtue, or left to run the wild career of uncontrolled passion, that we behold the good man or the bad. Hence, although we ought to cultivate our particular talents and inclinations, as it is only in this our natural sphere that we can figure with eclat, yet we should be particularly careful not to suffer them to lead us into excess; for what in moderation is innocent, or even a virtue, may, in its extreme, become a vice. Thus the painful and industrious man of business should take care he becomes not a miser, or dishonestly cunning; the lively and generous, that they become not rakes and spendthrifts; and the amorous, that they sink not into lewdness and debauchery.

Every one is ready to condemn those vices of which he thinks himself free, but would fain excuse those of which he knows he has his share. We are all like the honest parish clerk, who gave his hearty amen to all the anathemas of the Commination, until the parson pronounced " Cursed is he who lieth with his neighbour's wife ;" to which, for certain private reasons, being unwilling to give his assent, he deliberately and prudently rejoined, " Nay—a—a —then."

We are but too apt to give indulgence to those passions which are our favourites, and think it some amends to keep free from those vices, to which we have no inclination. We would fain believe that the gratifying one folly cannot condemn, and yet, perhaps, in this lies our whole trial. If, by the kindness of Heaven, I have an honest means of procuring

the

the neceffaries of life, and fo much found common fenfe, as to value riches only as they are really ufeful, what merit is it in me that I do not covet or fteal? And, if my temper be not irafcible, and no man has malicioufly injured me, what fhould make me hate or injure another? But if I have fome darling appetite to gratify, and to pleafe it facrifice every confideration of prudence, juftice, and religion, am I not (fo far as it has pleafed Heaven to try me) a foolifh, immoral, and impious man?

By keeping our paffions under due control, they become every day lefs troublefome : but, by indulgence, they as daily gather ftrength, and if they be allowed their full length of rein, they will foon lead us into fuch exceffes, they will fo warp our reafon as to make us at laft unfeeling, and render us guilty of fuch actions, as, in our more innocent ftate, we would have fhuddered at the very thoughts of. We become not only hardened in our firft kind of fin, but one vice is often introductory of others ; and we are led, nay almoft compelled, to commit fuch crimes as are moft repugnant to our natural difpofitions, and diftreffing to the feelings of our own hearts.

Thus are the generous and kind, by running into extravagances, and fo involving themfelves in difficulties and diftrefs, forced to become mean, fawning, deceitful, and unjuft ; and into what fhocking fcenes of lewdnefs or cruelty, has not drunkennefs led the naturally virtuous and good-natured man?

Virtue is of herfelf fo lovely, and vice fo naturally loathfome, to the human heart, that no man methinks could endure the confcioufnefs of wanting the one, and fhame of being flave to the other, did we not deceive ourfelves by giving falfe names to things. Thus extravagance is called contempt of avarice, and avarice diflike to luxury and wafte. Lewdnefs is called gallantry, and drunkennefs good fellowfhip ;

or elfe we draw a veil over our own deformity of manners, by making partial comparifons betwixt ourfelves and others, as thinking it a kind of negative virtue, that we are not quite fo bad as they.

Another way people comfort themfelves under a confcioufnefs of their prefent iniquity is, by their hopes of future amendment ; but that vice which we will not or cannot conquer to-day, will be yet worfe to fubdue to-morrow. Paffion, by being indulged, continually gathers ftrength, while our power of refiftance muft naturally grow weaker. It is one great proof of the immortality of the human foul, that our paffions and defires decay not always with our bodily powers to gratify them. How will the fpirits of decrepid age revive, when talking of what was the darling pride or pleafures of youth ! How will the drunkard repine for liquors, now become taftelefs in his mouth ; and the lafcivious man

" Still to his miftrefs hie with feeble knees !"

It is this confideration which has induced fome, with great reafon, to believe, that it will be in extremity of thefe never-to-be-gratified, thefe ever-longing defires, that the future punifhment of the wicked is to confift : this, with the confcious dread of an offended God, a mind robbed of every hope, of every virtue, and tortured with malicious envy, rage, and defpair, will be indeed a worm which never *never* dies.

BENEFITS OF INDUSTRY

An idle man is the Devil's playfellow.

IT is the duty of every man to purfue fome employment which may be beneficial to himfelf and his family, or to the community of which he is a member:

ber. Indeed the bulk of mankind are compelled to this from neceffity ; for there are comparatively few whofe circumftances are independent. But even thofe who are in the moft elevated fituations, ought to employ themfelves in fervices to their friends, their dependants, and their country. The rich cannot be fupported without the labours of the poor, and it is unreafonable that they fhould derive fuch confidera-ble advantages from the induftry of others, without fome efforts to promote the happinefs of thofe, by whofe labour they are benefited.

On thefe principles, and from a conviction that idlenefs was injurious to the conftitutions and morals of men, and very unjuft and mifchievous to fociety, the ancient Greeks and Romans appointed magif-trates to fee that no perfon fpent their time in floth ; and feverely punifhed thofe that thus offended. It was the general cuftom of the Jews to bring up their children to manual labour, how plentiful foever their circumftances were, or how polite foever their education was defigned to be. On this account we find the Apoftle Paul, who had a learned education, under the greateft of their rabbies, working as a tent-maker. The fame cuftom is continued in other na-tions to this day.

A diligent application to fome ufeful employment is a great prefervative againft vice, and a guard againft temptations of various kinds. It is hardly poffible, that any man fhould continue abfolutely unemploy-ed for a long time ; and he that is not doing what he ought, will be doing what he ought not. An honeft diligence fubdues thofe fenfual difpofitions which are cherifhed by floth and indolence.

But diligence has not only a tendency to prevent evil, but is naturally productive of the greateft advan-tages*. Many things, which at firft fight appear
beyond

_____

* The hand of the diligent maketh rich. PROV. x, 4.

beyond our reach, are furmountable by perfevering labour and induftry. What cannot be done by *one* ftroke is effected by many ; and application and perfe-verance have often fucceeded, even where all other means have failed ; by repeated efforts we may com-pafs in the end, what in the beginning we were. rea-dy to defpair of.

------◦◦◦------

ON CONJUGAL LOVE :

A FRAGMENT.

IN wedlock the loofer paffions of youth are con-folidated into a fettled affection; for the lawful object of love unites every care in itfelf ; and makes even thofe thoughts that were painful before, become de-lightful. When two minds are thus engaged by the ties of reciprocal efteem, each alternately receives and communicates a tranfport that is inconceivable to all, but thofe that are in this fituation ; from hence arifes that heart-ennobling folicitude for one another's welfare,that tender fympathy that alleviates affliction, and that participated pleafure that heightens profper-ity and joy itfelf.

This is a full completion of the bleffings of human-ity ; for if reafon and fociety are the characteriftics which diftinguifh us from other animals ; an excel-lence in thefe two great privileges of man, which centres in wedlock, muft raife us in happinefs above the reft of our fpecies.

It is here that the nobleft paffions of which the human foul is fufceptible join together, virtuous love and friendfhip ; the one fupplying it with a conftant rapture, and the other regulating it by the rules of reafon. . . . .

------◦◦◦------

EVENING.

EVENING.

AN ELEGY.

THE parting fun reflects its ev'ning ray,
And giant fhadows variegate the ground;
The wanton kids forfake their harmlefs play,
And folemn filence reigns the vale around.

Now fancy leads her airy-plumed train.
Through mazy walks by gently-purling rills,
Now Philomela fwells her mournful ftrain,
And all the grove with foftelt mufic fills.

Here, mofs-grown grots and bubbling ftreams are feen,,
And gloomy groves in ftately columns rife ;
Here fruitful meads enamell'd all with green,
There awful mountains feem to prop the fkies.

Now Cynthia gilds the dew-befpangled grove,
And cafts profufely round her maiden light ;
Led by the mufe, thro' filent paths I'll rove,
And pleafe my fancy with the varied fight.

Behold that rock that rears its head fo high,
In rude magnificence o'erlooks the flood ;
See on its top the mangled ruins lie,
Where once a caftle's ftately turrets ftood.

The creeping ivy fhades each tottering tower,
And clafps the ruins with a fond embrace ;
The fcreech-owls claim their melancholy bower,
And boding ravens hover round the place.

How vain the pageantry of worldly things !
And what is grandeur, but an empty name ?
Short-liv'd the glory of the greateft kings,
Though flaughter'd nations raife their ill-got fame..

H 2   Where

Where is, alas ! the pride of Perſia flown ?
   The pomp of Rome, with all her empire's o'er,
And e'en where Ilium ſtood, is ſcarcely known,
   And haughty Carthage now exults no more !

Thus, ſince Ambition yields her certain fate,
   By Reaſon prompted, ſure, unerring guide ;
Let Virtue bleſs thy viſionary ſtate,
   Whoſe glory, Time nor Envy ne'er can hide.

ALCANDER;

OR, THE

RECLUSE.

AN ELEGY.

FOE to the world's purſuit of wealth and fame,
   Alcander early from the world retir'd,
Left to the buſy throng each boaſted aim,
   Nor aught, ſave peace in ſolitude, deſir'd.

Foe to the futile manners of the proud,
   He choſe an humble virgin for his own ;
A form with Nature's faireſt gifts endow'd,
   And pure as vernal bloſſoms newly blown.

Her hand ſhe gave, and with it gave a heart,
   By love engag'd, with gratitude impreſt,
Free without folly, prudent without art,
   With wit accompliſh'd, and with virtue bleſt.

                        Swift

Swift pafs'd the hours; alas, to pafs no more!
Flown like the thin clouds of a fummer's day;
One beauteous pledge the lov'd Eliza bore,
The fatal gift forbad the giver's ftay.

O the dread fcene! 'Tis agony to tell,
How o'er the couch of pain reclin'd my head;
And took from dying lips the long farewell,
The laft, *laft* parting, ere her fpirit fled.

Reftore her, Heav'n! for once in mercy fpare;
Thus Love's vain prayer in anguifh interpos'd;
And foon Sufpenfe gave place to dumb Defpair,
And o'er the paft, Death's fable curtain clos'd.

O lovely flow'r, too fair for this rude clime;
O lovely morn, too prodigal of light!
O tranfient beauties, blafted in their prime;
O tranfient glories funk in fudden night!

Sweet Excellence, by all who knew thee mourn'd;
Where is that form, that mind, my foul admir'd;
That form, with every pleafing charm adorn'd,
That mind, with every gentle thought infpir'd?

The face with rapture view'd, I view no more;
The voice with rapture heard, no more I hear,
Yet the lov'd features Mem'ry's eyes explore;
Yet the lov'd accents fall on Mem'ry's ear.

TRUE

TRUE PLEASURE;

AN ESSAY.

Oh! how amiable is benevolence!

'THE man whose heart is replete with pure and unaffected piety, who looks upon the great Creator of the universe, in that juft and amiable light which all his works reflect upon him, cannot fail of tafting the fublimeft pleafure, in contemplating the ftupendous and innumerable effects of his infinite goodnefs.

Whether he looks abroad on the natural or moral world, his reflections muft ftill be attended with delight; and the fenfe of his own unworthinefs, fo far from leffening, will increafe his pleafure, while it places the forbearing kindnefs and indulgence of his Creator in a ftill more interefting point of view.

Here his mind may dwell upon the prefent, look back to the paft, or ftretch forward into futurity, with equal fatisfaction; and, the more he indulges contemplation, the higher will his delight arife. Such a difpofition as this, feems to be the moft fecure foundation, on which the fabric of true pleafure can be built.

Next to the veneration of the Supreme Being, the love of human kind feems to be the moft promifing fource of pleafure. And it is a never-failing one to him, who, poffeffed of this principle, enjoys all the power of indulging his benevolence; who makes the fuperiority of his fortune, his knowledge, or his power, fubfervient to the wants of his fellow-creatures around him.

It is true, there are few whofe power or fortune are fo adequate to the wants of mankind, as to render them capable of performing acts of *univerfal* benefi-

cence

cence; but a fpirit of univerfal benevolence may be poffeffed by all; and the bounteous Author of Nature has not proportioned the pleafure to the greatnefs of the effect, but to the greatnefs of the caufe.

The contemplation of the beauties of the univerfe, the cordial enjoyments of friendfhip, the tender delights of love, and the rational pleafures of religion, are open to all; and they each of them feem capable of giving real happinefs. Thefe being the only fountains, from which true pleafure fprings, it is no wonder that many fhould be compelled to fay they have not yet found it; and ftill cry out, " *Who will fhow us any good ?*" They feek it in every way but the *right* way : they want a heart for *devotion, humanity, friendfhip,* and *love,* and a tafte for what is truly beautiful and admirable.

ANECDOTES
OF THE LATE
MR. GAINSBOROUGH, THE PAINTER.

MR. GAINSBOROUGH, the landfcape-painter, was one of the greateft geniufes in his line that ever adorned any age or nation. His death was occafioned by a wen in the neck, which grew internally, and fo large as to obftruct the paffages. The effects of it became violent, a few months fince, from a cold caught one morning in Weftminfter-hall, at the trial of Mr. Haftings.

The malady began to increafe from this time; but its fymptoms fo much eluded the fkill of Dr. Heberden and Mr. John Hunter, that they declared it was nothing more than a fwelling in the glands, which the warm weather would difperfe. With this profpect
he

he went to his cottage near Richmond, where he remained for a few days ; but growing worfe, he returned.   A fuppuration taking place foon after, Mr. John Hunter acknowledged the protuberance to be a cancer.

Mr. Pott was at this time called in with Dr. Warren ; who confirmed this opinion, but found it impracticable to adminifter aid.   In a fituation thus defperate, the efteemed and admired Gainfborough languifhed and died ignorant of the malady which brought him to his end.   Since his death, the part has been opened, the excrefcence examined, and replaced.

Mr. Gainfborough was juft turned of fixty-one years of age.   He was born at Sudbury, in Suffolk, in 1727.   His father, on his outfet in life, was poffeffed of a decent competency ; but a large family, and a liberal heart, foon leffened his wealth.   His fon very early difcovered a propenfity to painting.   Nature was his teacher, and the woods of Suffolk his academy.   Here he would pafs in folitude his mornings, in making a fketch of an antiquated tree, a marfhy brook, a few cattle, a fhepherd and his flock, or any other accidental objects, that were prefented to his view.

From delineation he got to colouring ; and after painting feveral landfcapes from the age of ten to twelve he quitted Sudbury in his thirteenth year, and came to London, where he commenced portrait-painter ; and from that time never put his family to the leaft expenfe.   The perfon at whofe houfe he principally refided was a filverfmith of fome tafte ; and from him he was ever ready to confefs he derived great affiftance.

Mr. Gravelot, the engraver, was alfo his patron, and got him introduced at the old Academy of the Arts, in St. Martin's-lane.   He continued to exercife

cife his pensil in London for some years ; but mar-
rying while he was only *nineteen* years of age, he soon
after took up his residence at Ipswich ; and after
practising there for a confiderable period, went to
Bath, where, his friends intimated, his merits would
meet their proper reward.

VERSES
WRITTEN BY MR. CUNNINGHAM
TO AN
INTIMATE FRIEND,
ABOUT THREE WEEKS BEFORE HIS DEATH.

DEAR friend, as you run o'er my rhyme,
   And fee my long name at the end ;
You'll cry—" And has Cunningham time
   To give fo much verfe to his friend ?"

'Tis true, the reproof (tho' fevere)
   Is juft from the letters I owe ;
But blamelefs I ftill may appear,
   For nonfenfe is all I beftow.

However, for better or worfe,
   As Damons their Chloes receive ;
Ev'n take the dull lines I rehearfe,
   They're all a poor friend has to give.

The Drama and I have fhook hands,
   We've parted, no more to engage,
Submiffive I met her commands,
   For nothing can cure me of age.

                         My

My sunshine of youth is no more,
  My mornings of pleasure are fled !
With sorrow my fate I deplore,
  A pension supplies me with bread !

Dependant at length on the man
  Whose fortune I struggled to raise !
I conquer my pride as I can,
  His charity merits my praise !

His bounty proceeds from his heart ;
  'Tis principle prompts the supply ;
His kindness exceeds my desert,
  And often suppresses a sigh.

But like the old horse in the song,
  I'm turn'd on the common to graze ;
To Fortune these changes belong,
  And contented I yield to her ways !

She ne'er was my friend, through the day,
  Her smiles were the smiles of deceit ;
At noon she'd her favours display,
  And at night let me pine at her feet.

No longer her presence I court,
  No longer I shrink at her frowns !
Her whimsies supply me with sport,
  And her smiles I resign to the clowns !

Thus lost to each worldly desire,
  And scorning all riches and fame,
I quietly hope to retire,
  When death shall the summons proclaim.

THE

THE LAST MOMENTS

AND

HAPPY DEATH OF ROUSSEAU.

IN the afternoon of Wednefday, July 1, 1778, Rouffeau took his ufual walk with his *little governor*, as he called him : the weather was very warm, and he feveral times ftopped, and defired his little companion to reft himfelf (a circumftance not ufual with him), and complained, as the child afterwards related, of an attack of the colic ; which, however, was entirely removed when he returned to fupper, fo that even his wife had no fufpicion of his being out of order. The next day he arofe at his ufual hour, went to contemplate the rifing fun in his morning walk, and returned to breakfaft with his wife.

Some time after, at the hour fhe generally went out about her family bufinefs, he defired her to call and pay a fmith that had done fome work for him ; and charged her particularly to make no deduction from his bill, as he appeared to be an honeft man ; preferving to the laft moments of his life, thofe fentiments of probity and juftice which he enforced by his example, not lefs perfuafively than by his writings. His wife had been out but a few minutes, when returning fhe found him fitting in a ftraw chair, and leaning with his elbow on a neft of drawers.

" What is the matter with you, my dear ?" fays fhe : " do you find yourfelf ill ?"

" I feel," replies he, " a ftrange uneafinefs and oppreffion, befides a fevere attack of the colic."

Madam Rouffeau, upon this, in order to have affiftance without alarming him, begged the porter's wife to go to the chateau, and tell that her hufband was taken ill. Madame de Girardin, being the firft

I   whom

whom the news reached, hurried there inftantly, and as that was with her a very unufual hour of vifiting Roufleau, fhe, as a pretext for her coming, afked him and his wife, whether they had not been difturbed in the night by the noife made in the village.

"Ah! madam," anfwered Roufleau, in a tone of voice that declared the feeling he had of her con-defcenfion, "I am perfectly fenfible of your goodnefs, but you fee I am in pain, and to have you a witnefs of my fufferings, is an addition to them ; and both your own delicate ftate of health, and the natural ten-dernefs of your heart, unfit you for the fignt of other peoples fufferings. You will do me a kindnefs, and yourfelf too, Madam, by retiring, and leaving me a-lone with my wife for fome time."

She returned therefore to the chateau, to leave him at liberty to receive without interruption, fuch affift-ance as his colic required, the only affiftance, in ap-pearance, which he ftood in need of.

As foon as he was alone with his wife, he defired her to fit down befide him.

"Here I am, my dear (fays he) ; how do you find yourfelf?"

"The colic tortures me feverely, but I entreat you to open the window ; let me once more fee the face of nature : how beautiful it is ?"

"My dear hufband, what do you mean by faying fo ?"

"It has always been my prayer to God, (replied he with the moft perfect tranquility,) to die without doctor or difcafe, and that you may clofe my eyes : my prayers are on the point of being heard. If I have ever been the caufe of any affliction to you ; if by being united to me, you have met with any mis-fortune, that you would have otherwife avoided, I entreat your pardon for it."——

"Ah,

" Ah, it is my duty (cried she all in tears), it is *my* duty, and not your's, to ask forgiveness for all the trouble and uneasiness I have occasioned to you! But what can you mean by talking in this manner?"

" Listen to me, my dear wife, I feel that I am dying, but I die in perfect tranquility: I never meant ill to any one, and I firmly hope and rely on the mercy of God. My friends have promised me never to dispose, without your consent, of the papers I have put into their hands; the Marquis de Girardin will have the humanity to claim the performance of their promise. Thank the marquis and his lady on my part; I leave you in their hands, and I have sufficient dependance on their friendship, to carry along with me the satisfactory certainty, that they will be a father and mother to you. Tell them I request their permission to be buried in their garden, and that I have no choice as to the particular spot. Give my *souvenir* to my little Governor, and my Botany to Mademoifelle Girardin. Give the poor of the village something to pray for me, and let the honest couple whose marriage I had fettled, have the present I intended to make them. I charge you besides, particularly to have my body opened after my death, by proper persons, and that an exact account of the appearances and dissection be committed to writing."

In the mean time the pains he felt increased; he complained of shooting pains in his breast and head. His wife being no longer able to conceal her affliction, he forgot his own sufferings to console her.

" What! (said he,) have I lost all your affection already; and do you lament my happiness, happiness never to have an end, and which it will not be in the power of men to alter or interrupt? See how clear the heavens look, (pointing to the sky, in a kind of transport that seemed to collect all the energy of his soul;) there is not a single cloud. How pure and

serene

ferene is this day ! O how grand is nature ! See that fun, whofe fmiling afpect calls me : behold yourfelf that immenfe light. There is God ; yes, God himfelf who opens for me his bofom, and invites me at laft to tafte that eternal and unalterable peace which I had fo eagerly defired."

At thefe words he fell forwards, dragging his wife down along with him. Attempting to raife him, fhe found him fpeechlefs and without motion. Her cries brought all within hearing to her affiftance ; the body was taken up and laid on the bed. At that moment I entered, and taking his hand, I found it ftill warm, and then imagined his pulfe beat ; the fhortnefs of the time in which the fatal event had taken place, the whole having paffed in lefs than a quarter of an hour, left me a ray of hope. I fent for the neighbouring furgeon, and difpatched a perfon to Paris for a phyfician, a friend of Rouffeau's, charging him to come without a moment's delay. I called for fome *alkali volatile fluor*, and made him fmell to, and fwallow it repeatedly, all to no effect. The confummation fo delightful to him, and fo fatal to us, was already completed ; and though his example taught me how to die, it could not teach me to bear his lofs without heartfelt forrow and concern.

Like other tyrants, Death delights to fmite,
What fmitten, moft proclaims the pride of power
And arbitrary nod. NIGHT THOUGHTS.

AN

INDIAN KING's ADVICE

TO HIS

S O N,

ON HIS

DYING BED.

M Y fon (faid the expiring monarch), the angel of death is now approaching, and in a few moments a breathlefs carcafe will be all that remains of
the once powerful Kalahad.   Remember, therefore,
my fon, that thou muft now govern this mighty empire alone.   Remember, O youthful monarch of Indoftan, that thy example will influence multitudes of
people ; it will conftitute either their happinefs, or
mifery.

If thou art careful to direct thy paths by the precepts of reafon, and to liften to the dictates of confcience ; if thou art indefatigable in punifhing opprefl-
ors, and thofe who wallow in wickednefs, and careful
to encourage virtue and merit wherever they are
found ; then fhall happinefs dwell in thy palaces, and
plenty fmile around thy habitations.   Treachery
fhall be banifhed from the empire of Indoftan, and
rebellion feek refuge in the dark caverns of the mountains. The tongue of the hoary fage fhall blefs thee,
and the fhepherd, as he tends his flocks in the paf-
tures of the Ganges, rehearfe the glories of thy reign.

Thus fhall thy life glide on ferenely ; and when
the angel of death receives his commiflion to put a
period to thy exiftence, thou fhalt receive the fummons with tranquility, and pafs without fear the
gloomy valley that feparates time from eternity ; for
remember, my fon, this life is nothing more than a

I 2   fhort

short portion of duration, a prelude to another that will never have an end.

It is a state of trial, a period of probation ; and as we spend it either in the service of virtue or vice, our state in the regions of eternity will be happy or miserable.

Farewel, my son, I am arrived at the brink of the precipice that divides the regions of spirits from those inhabited by mortals : treasure up the instructions of thy dying father in thy breast ; practice them, and be happy.

TRUE FRIENDSHIP

HAPPILY

POURTRAYED.

A world in purchase of a friend is gain.
NIGHT THOUGHTS.

THE best method to cultivate true friendship is by letting it, in some measure, make itself ; a similitude of minds or studies, and even sometimes a diversity of pursuits, will produce all the pleasures that arise from it. The current of tenderness widens, as it proceeds ; and two men imperceptibly find their hearts glowing with good-nature for each other, when they were at first perhaps only in pursuit of a little mirth or relaxation.

Plautinus was a man who thought that every good was to be purchased by riches ; and as he was possessed of great wealth, and had a mind formed for virtue, he resolved to gather a circle of the best men round

round him. Among the number of his dependants was Mufidorus, with a mind juft as fond of virtue, yet not lefs proud than his patron..

His circumftances, however, were fuch as forced him to ftoop to the good offices of his fuperior; and he faw himfelf daily among a number of others, loaded with benefits and proteftations of friendfhip. Thefe, in the ufual courfe of the world, he thought it prudent to accept; but, while he gave his efteem, he could not give his heart.

A want of affection often broke out in the moft trifling inftances, and Plautinus had fkill enough to obferve the minuteft actions of the man he wifhed to make his friend. In thefe he ever found his aim difappointed; for Mufidorus claimed an exchange of *hearts*, which Plautinus, folicited by a variety of other claims, could never think of beftowing.

It may be eafily fuppofed, that the referve of our poor proud man was foon conftrued into ingratitude.

Wherever Mufidorus appeared, he was remarked as the ungrateful man; he had accepted favours, it was faid, and ftill had the infolence to pretend to independence. The event, however, juftified his conduct. Plautinus, by mifplaced liberality, at length became poor, and it was then Mufidorus firft thought of making a friend of him.

He flew to the man of diffipated fortune, with an offer of all he had; wrought under his direction with affiduity; and, by uniting their talents, both were at length placed in that eafy ftate of life from which one of them had fo unhappily fallen.

If anxious cares are ruling in the breaft,
And oft deprive the mind of wonted reft,
The real friend will bear a willing part,
And foothe the care with fympathizing heart.

————◦◦◦————

THE

PLEASURES

AND

BENEFITS

OF

FRIENDSHIP.

Where heart meets heart reciprocally foft,
Each other's pillow to repofe divine.

NIGHT THOUGHTS.

FRIENDSHIP is a union of hearts by the,
means of virtue and merit, and confirmed by a certain refemblance and conformity of manners.   A,
brilliant wit, folid and agreeable talents, may gain
upon our efteem, but they have no right to our
friendfhip, unlefs they are accompanied with virtue.
We ought to diftinguifh that which pleafes now and
then, from that which will pleafe always.   We muft
behave with gentlenefs and politenefs to thofe with
whom we are to live, becaufe we cannot have too
many people to wifh us well ; but we are not to take
the meafures of a lafting friendfhip with any man except with one, who has a generous noble mind, as
well as a found judgment.   Caution and management are abfolutely neceflary in the choice of our
friends ; and we muft not deliver ourfelves up, upon
a *flight* acquaintance.   Friendfhips fuddenly formed,
commonly end as foon as they are begun.

One of the chief benefits of friendfhip, is, to com-
municate.fome fecret charm to every thing that happens in the life of a friend, whether good or bad ;
fomething that may leffen the fenfe of the bad, and
                                        raife

raife the fenfe of the good; fo that no misfortune may be infupportable, nor any pleafure loft-to him.

It confifts alfo in fetting us right in our notions, in correcting our falfe fteps, in favouring our enterprifes, in making us moderate in our fucceffes, and fupporting us in our adverfity. We muft excufe the faults of our friends; for to expect that our friends fhall have no faults, is as much as to refolve to have friendfhip with nobody.

If the reputation of our friends is attacked in their abfence, we muft engage in their defence; if they are prefent, we muft fecond them with prudence; and in private, we ought to have the courage to reprehend them for their faults.

Among true friends, there muft be no fuch thing as diftruft; there muft be no fecrets, except thofe which have been confided in you by a third perfon; which is a facred truft you are not to divulge upon any confideration whatfoever. Let the ties of friendfhip be ever fo ftrict, yet they have their bounds, and they muft be fubfervient to three principal duties. We are all born fubject to certain obligations; we owe a duty to God, to our country, and laft of all to our family. Thefe feveral duties have their different degrees; thofe of friendfhip are in the *laft* rank. As creatures we belong to one great Creator; as fubjects, to the ftate; and as men, to our families. We are born creatures, fubjects, and kinfmen, but we become friends. We come into the world charged with thefe firft debts, which we are obliged to pay; preferably to thofe which we contract by our own choice.

There are accidents not to be forefeen, which often break friendfhip. In this cafe, we muft take care of being too eafy in liftening to bad fuggeftions, too rigorous to condemn. Reafon and juftice forbid us to condemn any perfon without hearing; by a much ftronger reafon, common fenfe and humanity exact

it

it of us in the cafe of a friend. We fhould, on the contrary, with great coolnefs, examine into the truth, and above all, avoid making ufe of any fevere terms in coming to an eclairciffement; there are fome who, for want of this difcretion alone, have given wounds to the heart of a friend, which are never to be cured. If after all, one fhould be under an indifpenfable neceffity of breaking off entirely, there are meafures to be kept even in cafe of fuch a rupture. There is a refpect to be paid to paft friendfhip, at the time that it is no more. All noife and eclat muft particularly be avoided, and we ought to take fpecial care that this rupture is neither begun nor followed by paffion. Above all, we are not to difcover former fecrets. The myfteries of ancient friendfhip muft never be profaned.

To conclude :—happy is he who can find a true friend, and happy is he who poffeffes the true qualities neceffary to make a friend.

REFLECTIONS ON MARRIAGE.

To wed or not to wed, that is the queftion.

MARRIAGE is not only a matter of pofitive inftitution, and of moral obligation, but even of natural inftinct alfo. This latter article I fhall endeavour to prove, by the means of a certain phyfical peculiarity, which fo happily and remarkably diftinguifhes man from brute. Women may be wives throughout the year; other females can be miftreffes but for a feafon. This particular, in my opinion, amounts pretty nearly to a proof, that Providence, in the great fcheme and œconomy of the intellectual fyf-

tem,

tem, defigned men and women for *pairs* only, and not to be at liberty to range unbounded, like the beftial herd. This may be permitted to the *bull*, the *buck*, the *ram*, &c. to anfwer the wife purpofes of nature ; but man is under no fuch natural neceffity for change.

No condition for a man feems more natural than that of *marriage ;* it is the fole end for which his whole frame and contexture feem calculated ; all his fenfes, with an imperceptible violence, draw him into this union ; an union which if entered into under the aufpices of religion and reafon, and cemented by a fimilarity of tempers, proportion of ages, and cherifhed by mutual complaifance, is productive of the moft folid happinefs ; but where intereft or paffion join their hands, where jarring fentiments and mutual neglects alienate the heart, it is, and ever will be, productive of real evils.

There is, however, no ftate which is entitled to more efteem and honour ; yet of all, perhaps, it meets with the leaft ; this difappointment is owing to the fpread of debauchery which has eclipfed its dignity, and decries it as a gulf of inevitable dangers ; thus being dreaded, it is defpifed and fhunned. Notwithftanding, if marriage be beneficial to mankind at large, it muft evidently be fo for individuals ; the good of the whole being the fame with the good of all its parts.

The inconveniences of a fingle life are in a great meafure neceffary and certain ; but thofe of the conjugal ftate are accidental and avoidable. Of all who marry, there are few who have any other view than their own perfonal gratification ; intereft promotes marriage with the old, and paffions quickly procure matches for the young. On either fide there is neither love nor efteem, and from thefe alone muft be derived true happinefs : therefore, it is from the general

eral folly of mankind, that their difcontent in marriage arifes; they make a rafh choice without judgment or forefight; without inquiring into the conformity there is (or fhould be) of opinions, the fimilarity of manners, rectitude of judgment, or purity
of fentiments, and are, confequently, unhappy when
it is made.

A young man and woman meet by chance, or are
brought together by defign : they exchange glances
and civilities : they go home and dream of one another; having little to divert attention or diverfify
thought, they find themfelves uneafy when they are
apart, and therefore conclude they fhall be happy
together; they marry, and difcover what nothing
but voluntary blindnefs had before concealed; they
wear out their days with altercations,& charge nature
with cruelty.   Surely all thefe evils might be avoided, by that deliberation and forethought which prudence prefcribes to a choice for life.

Upon the whole, a married life is always an *infipid*,
a *vexatious*, or an *happy* condition; the firft is, when
two people of no genius or tafte meet together, upon
fuch a fettlement as has been thought reafonable by
parents and conveyancers, from an exact valuation of
the lands and cafh of both parties; in this cafe, the
young lady's perfon is no more regarded than the
houfe, and the improvements, in the purchafe of an
eftate.   But fhe goes with her fortune, rather than
her fortune with her; thefe make up the crowd,
or the vulgar of the rich, and fill up the number of the human race, without beneficence to thofe
below them, or refpect to thofe above them; and lead
a defpicable, independent, and ufelefs life, without
fenfe of the laws of kindnefs, good-nature, mutual offices, and the elegant fatisfactions which flow from
reafon and good fenfe.

                                        The

The vexatious married life arifes from a conjunction of two people of quick tafte and refentment, put together for reafons belt known to their friends ; in which efpecial care is taken to avoid (what they think the chief of evils) *poverty,* and enfure to them riches with every want befides. Thefe good people live in a conftant reftraint before company, and too great a familiarity when alone. When they are within obfervation, they fret at each other's carriage and behaviour ; when alone they revile each other's perfon and conduct ; in company they are in purgatory, when by themfelves, in hell.

The happy marriage is where two perfons meet and voluntarily make choice of each other, without principally regarding or neglecting the circumftances of fortune or beauty. Thefe may ftill love, in fpite of adverfity or ficknefs : the former we may in fome meafure defend ourfelves from ; the other is the common lot of humanity ; when efteem and love unite hearts, oftentation and pomp of living will not be coveted; folitude and mediocrity with the perfon beloved, yield true pleafure far beyond what can be derived from fhow and fplendour; mental perfections are the only folid foundations for conjugal happinefs ; the gifts of fortune are adventitious, and may be acquired, but intrinfic worth is permanent and incommunicable.

K   RULES

RULES FOR CHUSING A WIFE,

AND FOR,

BEHAVIOUR AFTER MARRIAGE.

WRITTEN BY A BATCHELOR.

THE firſt rule I have ſet to myſelf, is this, if ever I change my preſent way of life, I will prefer neither beauty, nor fortune, to good-humour and ſenſe. Thoſe, as a poet of our own finely ſays will ever laſt, when beauty may, nay *muſt* fade; and fortune alone will have no power to make life eaſy, without the other two.—But, ſecondly, I will endeavour to chuſe one, who, if ſhe be not a beauty, is at a pretty good diſtance from deformity; for, though it is commonly enough ſaid, and in ſome meaſure it may be true, that fancy ſurpaſſes beauty; yet there is no more reaſon, that a man's fancy ſhould ſtigmatize his ſenſes, than that his patience (doubtleſs, to be tried enough without) ſhould bear the burden of perpetual ſarcaſms. The world is wide enough; and a man, who has lived to my years a batchelor, will have no need to run a double gantlet, where the wits of the age declare any one of them a ſufficient topic for ſatire.—Yet, if a homely piece of houſehold ſtuff ſhould fall to my lot, I would of all things take particular care, not to provoke the ſatire of my neighbours by any overweening reflections or compariſons. To be ſure, under ſuch a diſaſter, I would endeavour to ſecure ſome fiddle-faddle grace or other, to commute for my liberty: good ſenſe, or good houſe-
wifery;

wifery ; or good-humour, or fome other good thing, fhould excufe me to *myfelf*, at leaft ; and fo long as I find complaifance and content at home, my neighbour muft have very little to do, and muft approve him- felf a man of vaft deficiency, both of bufinefs and wifdom, who will go about to difturb the peace of one that never troubles his head with him, or any thing that belongs to him.

If I think my own wife handfomer, difcreeter, or a better houfewife than his, can it be any addition to my own happinefs, to endeavour to leffen his, by ac- quainting him with my fentiments ? But on the con- trary, if I am confcious to myfelf that we are barely on a level in the matter, as to outward appearance at leaft ; what a laxnefs of tongue, or what an abfence of difcretion fhall I demonftrate, to triumph in ad- vantages, of which I cannot make others fenfible, without expofing myfelf to the cenfures and ill-natur- ed obfervations of thofe who perhaps would not, without fuch a provocation, ever have troubled their heads with me ? Sure the height of every man's real enjoyment muft be in his own domeftic content. He that pretends to be happy without it, deludes himfelf.   To enjoy our own with fatisfaction, and to rejoice in the fatisfaction of our neighbours, is an at- tainment at which very few arrive ; among whom thofe can never be reckoned, who endeavour to make others uneafy in their enjoyments, by a ridiculous of- tentation of their own.

ON

ON·POLITE BEHAVIOUR..

TRUE politeness is the greatest charm of civil' society; it teaches us to compassionate the errors and· weaknesses of· some, to bear with patience the whims and caprices of others, to give into their notions for· a while, in order to bring them· back afterwards to reason, by gentle and insinuating methods, accommodating ourselves to the humours of every body, from a real desire of pleasing in general.., With this view we assume every character and form that may possibly contribute to success; and though a long practice of complaisance be often a very disagreeable task with respect to people of a certain stamp, we, however, conquer our repugnance, and are not diverted from our pursuit by their untoward behaviour: however capricious people may be, it is very difficult for them not to be pleased with such persevering condescension and assiduity.

Politeness, likewise, directs us to decline the praises people may be willing to give us, and prompts us to bestow them liberally on others.. We are ingenious in expatiating on their amiable and excellent qualities: this is what makes us feel such exquisite and delicate pleasure in the company of· polite people of sentiment, judgment, and pliancy, who know how to accommodate themselves to our taste and dispositions.

It is rare to find so many accomplishments united; we must not, therefore, wonder that the number of. polite persons, is so comparatively small; ladies, who are naturally more mild, complaisant, and graceful than men, have likewise more politeness: and it is chiefly in an intercourse with them, that men learn
to

to be civil and polite, by studying to become agreeable to them*.

Polite manners render merit pleasing and lovely : whatever talents we may possess, the want of politenefs destroys the esteem which excellent qualities must otherwise produce. There are some who have a peculiar knack of heightening the folly or absurdity of others, as well as of exhibiting impertinent behaviour in a new light : this talent is the very reverse of politenefs ; which is indulgent to every body, and which always finds arguments to palliate the conduct of others, or at least to justify their intentions.

Polite persons have likewise great addrefs for entering into the taste and disposition of people ; for coming at the nature and extent of their capacity, and giving them opportunities of displaying their different abilities, they are lefs attentive to shine in conversation by engroffing it entirely to themselves, than to make the merit of others appear more conspicuous.

ON THE PRIDE OF HIGH BIRTH.

Let high birth triumph! what can be more great ?
Nothing--but merit---in a *low* estate. DR. YOUNG.

OF all the absurd circumstances by which the mind of man becomes elated, furely that of being defcended from great or titled ancestors is the most ridiculous ;

K 2

---

* Would to God this was *always* the pleasing confequence of intercourfe between the sexes.

diculous ; it is impoffible to value ourfelves on any
thing _lefs_ meritorious, or that more difplays the vanity of the human character ; moft other kinds of pride
have fome plea to give them countenance, but this
has none.   Riches fome may pride themfelves in, becaufe they give independence ; beauty and drefs may
procure admiration ; and efteem will always await
on intellectual accomplifhments..   But to be defcended from even the moft virtuous characters can never
be confidered as an advantage by the judicious part
of mankind, unlefs their good qualities, as well as
names, were hereditary ; nay, fo far from giving any
room to boaft, it muft certainly be a great mortification to many, to reflect how much they fall fhort of
the amiable character which the faithful pen of the
hiftorian has transmitted to pofterity.   They cannot
but know, that, to men of fenfe, the comparifon, or
rather contraft, muft appear difgraceful ; and that
their elevated rank, inftead of procuring them a part
of that refpect enjoyed by their progenitors, ferves
only to render them the more contemptible.

And as high birth can have no reafonable claim to
our reverence and efteem, when unaccompanied by
thofe qualities and difpofitions which make a man
truly great ; fo to defpife a man, merely for the
meannefs of his extraction, fhows equally a want of
fenfe and found judgment, and is the peculiar characteriftic of little minds.   Yet, though the truth of
thefe obfervations is fufficiently obvious, though this
fpecies of pride is without the fhadow of a reafon to
fupport it, it is aftonifhing to think what an influence
it has over the conduct of the generality of people at
the prefent time.

No fooner does a perfon, arrived at a ftate of independence, by an exertion of his induftry only, appear
in any public fcene of life, but the bufy tongue of a
                                                  foolifh

foolifh curiofity is employed in an inquiry into his family; and, though he may have imbibed the moft virtuous principles, though his genius may be fuch as would render him a valuable acquifition to focie-ty, yet, if he cannot boaft of a long lift of honoura-ble names in his pedigree, he is immediately treated with a fupercilious indifference, and deemed unwor-thy to affociate with people of quality. But fhould he dare to carry his thoughts fo high, as to wifh an alliance by marriage with a family of that clafs, in-cited thereto by the tendereft and moft fincere at-tachment to an object not infenfible of his merit, and lefs influenced by that pride which cuftom has made fo powerful an obftacle to their happinefs, he muft not wonder if the indifference he before experi-enced is exchanged for contempt. So much for the folly of modern nobility, in valuing themfelves for their high birth, without refpect to real merit. None's truly great, but he who's truly good.

RATIONAL PROOFS
OF THE
SOUL's IMMORTALITY
AND A
FUTURE STATE. ℞

IN A LETTER TO A MODERN DEIST,
AN EXTRACT.

It muft be fo---Plato, thou reafon'ft well---.
Elfe whence this pleafing hope, this fond defire,
'I his longing after immortality ? . . . . .
'Tis heav'n itfelf that points out an hereafter,
And intimates eternity to man, ADDISON's CATO!

YOU acknowledge there is one felf-exiftent Being, and that from Him all derive their exiftence, whether *rational, animal, vegetable,* or *inanimate ;* from what we we see and know of his works, may we not reason with some degree of precision, by analogy, to what is less certainly understood ? Amongst all the works of creation, that come under our observation, is there any waste of powers, abilities, qualities, or properties ? Every plant can receive from that single spot, to which it is confined, all that is necessary for its support and nourishment ; it sickens by removal, and thrives in proportion to the close adhesion of its fibrous root to its mother *earth :* the power of motion, which would have been injurious, is therefore wisely denied.

Observe the various animals, see how their different powers, forms, qualities, and clothing are proportioned to their different natures, and the different occupations, or climates, they are destined to. Of what use to the mole would have been the eagle's eye, or to the horse the tiger's claw, feet to the fish, or fins to birds ? Not a superfluous gift is bestowed, but each species has exactly that form, construction, and those powers, which are most useful, necessary, and best suited to itself.

Let us then go on to examine *man* upon the same plan : Compare him with all the different kinds of animals over whom he claims, and exerts a sovereign power. Some of these are made his food, others necessary to the comfort and convenience of his life in different capacities ; neither of which could be obtained by the corporeal qualities he is endowed with, the brute creation being all, either by strength, swiftness, or the region they inhabit, beyond the reach of his arm.

The superior sagacity, therefore, which has enabled him to supply, by various arts, this natural defect of corporeal powers, was undoubtedly necessary to his subsistence ; because without it he would have been

the

the moſt defencelefs of all animals equal to himſelf
in ſize ; unable to procure the ſmaller kinds for his
food, and an eaſy prey to the larger.. Suppoſing
his whole duration to end with *this* life, or, at leaſt,
that no after-conſcioufnefs remains, was not.this ſort
of ſagacity, by which he braves the lion's force, bends
to the yoke the ſtubborn bullock's neck, breaks to the
curb the foaming ſteed, overtakes with certain death
the diſtant bird, or from the rapid ſtream· drags to
the ſhore the ſcaly· fry ; was not, I ſay, on ſuch a ſup-
poſition, this ſort of ſagacity, by which he reigns
acknowledged lord of this planet, ſufficient to anſwer
all the ends of. his creation ? Wherefore then this
waſte of *rational* powers ? this capacity of diving into
the philoſophical difference between matter and ſpirit ? of tracing effects up to their probable cauſes, and
accounting rationally for almoſt all the phenomena
of nature ?.

To what end is he endowed with the reaſoning faculty in a degree ſo ſuperior to his fellow-mortals
here, as to feel .(if the expreſſion may be allowed)
his derivation from ſome eternal exiſtence, and form
to himſelf not.only a wiſh, but even a probable proſ-
pect of immortality ? And that this is the reſult of
the natural powers of his mind, excluſive of any ſup-
poſed revelation, is evident from the conſtant, though
doubtful, hope of philoſophers in the earlieſt ages of
the world, from all the accounts that have been
tranſmitted to us.

Of what uſe to him, if conſcioufnefs·ends with reſ-
piration, is it to ſee ·and admire the eternal beauty
of truth, the fitnefs of things, the unalterable difference between·right and·wrong action, or moral good
and evil ; the beauty of·virtue, and the deformity of
vice ? And is it reaſonable to ſuppoſe, that in a world
wherein we ſee every creature below us exactly ſuit-
ed

ed to the manifeſt end of its creation, poſſeſſing juſt what is neceſſary and uſeful to it, and not a ſuperfluous gift beſtowed, that the Creator ſhould have been thus wantonly laviſh in the formation of *man* alone ; and ſtored his mind with uſeleſs faculties, in contradiction to the general plan of creation, which is evidently calculated for the utility, convenience, and happineſs of every other ſpecies ?

Admitting this to be his whole duration, how eminently wretched is he made by the ſuperior powers he boaſts of ! Every animal, in the different ſcales below himſelf, enjoys the preſent moment, unconſcious of futurity ; indulges every riſing wiſh, and fearleſs revels in every joy to which his inclination leads ; whilſt man, unhappy man ! for no end reſtrains his every paſſion by the ſevereſt rules of rigid reaſon ; and almoſt from the cradle to the grave, treads with trembling ſteps, as every moment on the verge of ruin ; in the deluſive hope of bringing his mind to a ſtate of ſuch perfection, as will qualify it for immortal happineſs, in that future exiſtence he is formed to expect. Should this expectation be vain, can the Being who interwove it in his nature be juſtly deemed benevolent, kind, or good ? if not, what are the attributes of the God you pretend to own ?

You ſay the word *immaterial* has no meaning, yet have you frequently aſſerted, that the ſoul is only a fine inviſible fluid, which being ſecreted from the brain, and diffuſed through the nerves, becomes the actuating principle ; I ſhould be glad to know what is to be underſtood by this ? To me it ſeems to imply a contradiction. By the word *inviſible* muſt be underſtood ſomething of a nature not to be diſcovered by our ſight : All *matter* is certainly the object of ſight. Give me leave to aſk how you came by the knowledge

ledge of this fine *invisible* fluid ? and by what means it acquires the power of thought, reflection, choice, and motion, properties that have never been supposed to belong to matter.

By the confcioufnefs which the immortal mind expects to carry with it into another world, and either to *fuffer* or *enjoy* for ever in fome future ftate of exif-tence, is meant an exact and indelible remembrance of all the paffions, affections, propenfities, actions, and inclinations of the mind, during the whole period in which it was united to matter. According to the nature of this retrofpect it muft unavoidably be pro-ductive of perfect happinefs or extreme mifery : The remembrance of having checked every propenfity, or rifing inclination, to vice*, and fo regulated every -affection, as to bring the mind into an habitual ftate of confcious purity, even in fentiment, muft afford that uninterrupted felicity, which confcious rectitude alone is capable of enjoying.

Should the mind, thus fupremely bleffed, behold the object of its tendereft love rendered irretrievably wretched by a retrofpect diametrically oppofite to its own, the deformity of the character muft raife a juft abhorrence ; while grateful pleafure would be more ftrongly excited at the thought of being removed to a ftate of exiftence, where vice no more could hide its hateful form, beneath the fair femblance of a vir-tuous garb.

Hermione was perhaps, the faireft of her fex ; A-draftus thought her foul as faultlefs as her face, in this opinion he held her neareft to his heart, and when the

---

* Happy would it be for men in general, did they endea-vour daily to maintain a confcience void of offence towards God and their fellow-creatures—but where is the man that does fo ?

the mandate for his diſſolution came, felt no reluc-
tant thought, but that of leaving this dear partner of
his joys behind—·Farewel, my love, he fainting cried,
'I go to wait thee in ſome better ſtate : haſte to rejoin
me, for till then, heaven can to me afford but an *imperfect* bliſs. ·Death ſnatched him from her arms.·
The mortal veil removed, the blaze of truth flaſhed
on his enlightened mind ;·he ſaw her, as ſhe really
was, a baſe, deſigning, artful hypocrite ; fled with
horror from the deteſted object, and bleſſed the moment that diſſolved their union here below.

Thus you ſee the happineſs of the good need not
to be interrupted by the puniſhment of the wicked.
Hermione ſinks to everlaſting ruin, beneath a load of
conſcious guilt, whilſt, Adraſtus, perfected in virtue,
mounts on high, and looks down with inward ſatisfaction and acquieſcence on the juſt reward of vice and
diſſimulation*.

THE

HERMIT OF THE MOUNTAINS,

AN EASTERN TALE.

Content alone is happineſs on earth.

The ſun had long ſince ſunk behind the adjacent
mountains, and the ſage Ibrahim was retiring to reſt,
when a knocking at the door of his hermitage drew
him thither ; he opened it, and there ſtood before
him

* Life and immortality, we are aſſured by God himſelf
in his word, are not brought to light by man's *reaſon* but
by the *Goſpel* ; there alone we may look for them with certainty, and be confirmed in the belief of them beyond a doubt.

him a youth, whofe care-marked vifage fpoke him to
be the child of grief : " Sire," faid the youth, " permit a ftranger to pafs the night beneath your friendly
roof, till the returning morn enables him to purfue
his way with fafety." The hermit bid him welcome
to his cot, and fpread his homely board before him.
Roots fupplied the place of coftly viands, and water
from a neighbouring fpring, the place of blood-inflam-
ing wine. The figh, the ftarting tear, and all the behaviour of his gueft, filled the fage with emotions of
compaffion ; and defiring, if poffible, to alleviate the
pains of the ftranger, he thus addreffed him :
" In a face fo young, in a breaft fo untutored
in this world's cares, it feems to me a wonder that
forrow is a gueft ; and might it not be thought a
bold intrufion, I would afk the fpring of thefe your
cares perhaps you mourn the pangs of difappointed
love, the lofs of fome dear friend or earthly joy.
Say, if your grief be of the common courfe, per-
chance my riper years may fpeak the wifhedfor comfort."—" Sire," replied the youth, " your kind
intentions demand at once my thanks and my com-
pliance.
" My father was a merchant ; in point of wealth,
Bagdad held not his equal ; early he left me to poffefs
his fortunes ; the lofs of my father was foon forgot
amidft the riches, flatterers, and friends, that now
furrounded me. But when reflaction took place, happinefs became my defire, and I vainly thought to be
rich was to be happy. I enlarged my merchandize,
I trafficked to all parts of the globe, and not a wind
blew into port, but it brought an increafe to my ftore ;
but yet I was not happy, my defiresincreafed with
my poffeffions, and I was yet miferable. I then determined to apply to *honour*, and there feek the happinefs riches would not afford me. I fold off my
L   wares,

wares, and by dint of friends and wealth, I foon obtained a commifllon, and on feveral occafions gave
proofs of my valour, till I was fent by the fovereign
to oppofe a rebellion that had broken out in a diftant
province.   I went, was fuccefsful, and returned in
triumph, laden with honours; and fo much was the
fultan poffeffed in my favour, that he offered me his
daughter in marriage.

"Awhile I thought myfelf happy : but the envy
of fome, and the artifice of others, foon convinced
me of my error.   I now refolved to quit public life,
and to feek in *pleafure* the happinefs hitherto unknown.
My palace now became the fcene of continued delights ; the richeft viands were daily on my table, the
moft coftly liquors fparkled in my bowl, and the
beauties of all nations adorned my feraglio : in fhort
my life was a continued round of pleafure.   But,
alas ! frequent debauchery impaired my health, and
the diverfions of the night embittered the reflections
of the morning.

" I now was determined to quit my home, and
feek in folitude and retirement, that happinefs I had
hitherto fought in vain, and which I am at times inclined to believe, is no more than the object of crea-
tive fancy.   For this purpofe I confIgned to the care
of a friend, all my poffeffions, and was on the fearch
after a proper place of retirement, when night overtook me and I implored the fhelter of your hofpita-
ble roof." Here paufed the youth, and thus the fage
began :

" The object of your purfuit, my fon, indeed is
good, and your not hitherto attaining it, arifes not
from its non-exiftence, but from your errors in the
purfuit of it.   Happinefs, my fon, has not its feat in
honour, pleafure, or *riches :* to be happy is in the power
of every individual ; to all, the great Supreme has

given

given wifely ; and thofe who receive what he gives with thankfulnefs and content, are the only happy.

" Return then, my fon, to thy poffeffions, employ the power of doing good lent by thy Creator, and know that contentment is the fubftance and happinefs her fhadow ; thofe who have the one, poffefs the other."

The words of the fage funk deep in the breaft of the ftranger ; he retired to reft in peace, and in the morn he returned again to his houfe, where he witneffed the truth of Ibrahim's advice : and embracing every method to do good, he lived in peace and tranquility ; and experienced that to be content is truly to be happy.

USEFUL OBSERVATIONS

ON THE

PASSIONS OF THE MIND.

BY AN EMINENT PHYSICIAN.

To maintain health, the paffions of the mind muft be kept under due fubjection. Let a perfon be ever fo temperate, and regular in his diet and exercife, yet if he is led away by his paffions, all his regularity will avail but little.

Fear, Grief, Envy, Hatred, Malice, Revenge, and *Defpair,* are known to weaken the nerves, retard the circulation, hinder perfpiration, impair digeftion, and to produce fpafms, obftructions, and hypochondriacal diforders.

Valarius Maximus gives fatal inftances of terror. Violent anger creates bilious, inflamatory, convulfive, and apoplectic diforders, efpecially in hot temperaments.

Pliny

Pliny and Aulus Gellies give us fatal inftances of extreme joy.

Sylla having freed Italy from eivil wars, returned to Rome. He faid, he could not fleep the firft night, his foul being tranfported with exceffive joy, as with a ftrong and mighty wind.

Thofe who brood over cares, are the firft attacked by putrid difeafes, and the hardeft to cure.

The hopes of ending their days among their native barren rocks, make the Switzers fight under any banner.

Africans tranfported to the colonies, no fooner caft their eyes on the hated fhores, than they refufe fuftenance, and often plunge into the main, from a notion that their departed fpirits regain their liberty.

Can drugs reach the feats of fuch difeafes ? What can medicines avail to love-fick minds ? Wounded fpirits who can bear ?

Moderate joy, virtue, contentment, hope, and courage, invigorate the nerves, accelerate the fluids, promote perfpiration, and affift digeftion.

Lord Verulam obferves, that cheerfulnefs of fpirits is particularly ufeful when we fit down to meals or go to reft. " If any violent paffions fhould furprife us at thefe feafons, it would be prudent to defer eating, or going to bed, until the mind recovers its natural tranquillity."

It is obfervable, that the perfpiration is larger from any vehement paffion of the mind, when the body is quiet, than from the ftrongeft bodily exercife, when the mind is calm and compofed. Hence we infer, that thofe who are prone to anger cannot bear much exercife, becaufe the exuberant perfpiration of both, might wafte the ftrength too faft.

DESCRIPTION.

DESCRIPTION OF A
COUNTRY WORK-HOUSE.

A FRAGMENT.

BEHOLD yon houfe that holds the parifh poor,
Whofe walls of mud fcarce bear the broken door ;
There, where the putrid vapours flagging play,
And the dull wheel hums doleful thro' the day*,
Children are plac'd who know no parent's care :
Parents, who know no children's love dwell there ;
Heart broken matrons on their joylefs bed,
Forfaken wives, and mothers never wed †;
Dejected widows with unheeded tears,
And crippled age with more than childhood fears ;
The lame, the blind, and, far the happieft they !
The moping idiot, and the madman gay‡.

Here too the fick their final doom receive,
Here brought amidft the fcenes of woe to grieve ;
Here forrowing, they their hours of trouble fcan,
And the cold charities of man to man ;
Whofe parifh laws for ruin'd age provide,
While ftrong compulfion plucks the fcarp from
pride ;

L 2   But

---

* The fpinning-wheel.

† The fcenes of mifery and diftrefs generally exhibited
in parifh work-houfes both in town and country, whether
occafioned by unavoidable misfortunes, or the effects of vice,
diffipation, or extravagance, are but fo many melancholy
pictures of the vanity, folly, and uncertainty of all human
expectations and purfuits.

‡ If (as it is often faid) there are pleafures in madnefs
which none but madmen know, I am well affured they are
unenvied in the enjoyment of them.

But ſtill that ſcarp is bought with many a ſigh,
And pride embitters what it can't deny.
 Say ye, oppreſt by ſome *fantaſtic* woes,
(Some jarring nerve that baffles your repoſe ?)
Who with ſad prayers the weary doctor teaze,
To name the namelefs ever new diſeaſe.;
Who with mock patience dire complaints endure,.
Which *real* pain and that alone can cure *;
How. would ye bear in *real* pain to lie ;.
Deſpis'd, neglected, left alone to die ?
How would ye bear to draw your lateſt breath;
Where all that's wretched paves the way for death?
 Such is that room which one rude beam divides,
And naked rafters form the ſloping ſides :
Where the vile bands that bind the thatch are ſeen,
And lathes and mud are all that lie between,
Save one dull pane that coarſely patch'd, gives way,
To the rude tempeſt, yet excludes the day :
Here, on a matted flock, with duft o'erſpread,
The drooping wretch reclines his languid head.
For him no hand the cordial cup applies,
Nor wipes the tear that ſtagnates in his eyes ;
No friends with foft diſcourſe his pains beguile,
Nor promiſe hope till ſicknefs wears a ſmile†..
But with bare neceſſaries ſcarce ſupply'd,

And

---

* How many among the noble and affluent parts of mankind are there, who having no *real* troubles to perplex them,
make to themſelves *imaginary* ones, and conſequeatly become their own tormentors ? Such perſons deſerve no pity.

† However ſurrounding friends may not be able, when we
are afflicted, to remove our pains ; their ſympathy and con-
verſe may tend greatly to alleviate them ; well therefore does
a late eminent writer ſay,
 " Poor is the friendlefs maſter of a world."
DR. YOUNG.

And rack'd with pain he turns from fide to fide;
At evening longing for the morning light,
And wifhing every morning it was night,

. . . .
Such fcenes of dire diftrefs, 'tis but too true, ·
A parifh workhoufe oft prefents to view †.

A REAL CHRISTIAN DELINEATED. ·

Chriftian is the higheft ftyle of man:

NIGHT THOUGHTS.

IF a man is proud· and ambitious, he cannot be
of the true church of Chrift ; for Chrift was lowly,
meek, and humble. If a·man is cruel, he cannot be
of that church ; for Chrift was tender-hearted. If
a man is unforgiving and revengeful, he cannot be
of that church ; for Chrift forgave his·enemies, and
prayed for them. If you are avaricious,·you cannot be of that church ; for Chrift defpifed riches. If
you are vain-glorious, you cannot be of that church ;
for Chrift fought not the praife of man; but the
glory of God. If you· know your brethren to . be
in diftrefs, and affift them not (if it is in your power
to do it), you cannot be of that church ; for Chrift
comforted the afflicted, relieved the needy, healed
the fick,·and even gave his life to fave his enemies
from deftruction.

If

† It is too true an obfervation,that there are very few if any
of the excellent public charities the metropolis abounds with
but what are abufed ; the farming of the poor, as it is generally ftyled, has been the inlet to many flagrant abufes,
and therefore fhould not be allowed.

If you are envious, you cannot be of that church; for Chrift envied no man's happinefs. If you pafs rafh or evil judgment on the actions of your neighbour, you cannot be of that church; for Chrift judged none unfavourably. If you are luftful, you cannot be of that church; for Chrift had no unclean defires. If you are a curfer, or fwearer, you cannot be of that church; for Chrift took not the name of God in vain. If you are a drunkard, or a glutton, you cannot be of that church; for Chrift was moderate in all things‡.

If you are a liar, you cannot be of that church; for Chrift always fpoke truth, though he fuffered for it. If you are contentious, you cannot be of that church; for Chrift was a peace-maker. If you are an idler, you cannot be of that church; for Chrift employed his time well, daily going about doing good. If you are a thief, or an unjuft dealer, you cannot be of that church; for Chrift rendered Cæfar his due. If you are a felf-lover, you cannot be of that church*; for Chrift loved others better than himfelf, or he had not died for their fakes.

We are apt to fet too great a value on the few good actions of our lives, and imagine one meritorious deed fufficient to over-balance numberlefs repeated crimes: but this is a great miftake, and the error of felfefteem; for it is not enough that we obey our mafter's commands in a few immaterial points, but we muft execute his orders ftrictly, in every particular, ere we can prove ourfelves his faith-

ful

---

‡ If we bear not the image of Chrift in our tempers, lives, and conduct, we cannot be his difciples; they only are his friends who do whatfoever he commandeth. John, xv. 14.

* A real Chriftian has the feeds of all thefe evils in his corrupt nature; but grace enables him to fubdue them.

ful fervents; In fhort, if we do not love God above all things, and our neighbours as ourfelves ; we are not of Chrift's church, nor in the leaft entitled to the benefits and blefings he hath promifed to them that love and ferve him † ! Alas! how few *real* Chriftians there are in the world !

THE REPRIEVED MALEFACTOR;

AN AFFECTING SCENE,

LATELY EXHIBITED IN NEWGATE.

-----" A dreadful din was wont
To grate the fenfe, when enter'd here, from groans,
And howls of flaves condemn'd : from clink of chains,
And crafh of rufty bars, and creeking hinges !
And ever and anon the light was dafh'd
With frightful faces, and the meagre looks
Of grim and ghaftly executioners." CONGREVE.

THE tolling of the dreadful bell, fummoning the miferable to pay their forfeited lives to the injured laws of their country, awoke Henry from the firft fleep he had fallen into, fince he entered the walls of a difmal prifon.

Henry had been a merchant, and married the beautiful Eliza in the midft of affluence ; but the capture of our Weft India fleet, in the late American

† It is not being of this, that, or the other fect or denomination among the profeffors of Chriftianity, that will conftitute a man a real Chriftian in God's account ; but his being poffeft of the love of Chrift in his heart, and evidencing it in his life and converfation in the world.

can war, was the firft ftroke his houfe received. His creditors, from the nature of the lofs, were for fome time merciful ; but to fatisfy fome partial demands, he entered into a diſhonourable treaty, which being difcovered, Henry was thrown into a loathfome goal. He had offended againſt the laws, and was condemned to die.

Eliza poffeffed Roman virtues. She would not quit his fide, and with her infant fon, ſhe preferred chafing away his melancholy in a dungeon, to her father's houfe, which was ſtill open to receive her. Their hopes of a reprieve from day to day, had fled; but not before the death-warrant arrived. Grief overpowering all other fenfes, Sleep, the balmy charmer of the woes of humanity, in pity to their miferies, extended her filken embraces over them, and beguiled the time they had appropriated for prayer ; and Eliza, with the infant, ſtill continued under her influence.

" Father of mercies," exclaimed Henry, " lend thine ear to a fupplicating penitent. Give attention to my ſhort prayer. Grant me forgivenefs, endue me with fortitude to appear before thee : and, O God! extend thy mercies to this injured, this beſt of thy fervants, on whom I have entailed undeferved heartfelt woe. Chace not fleep from her, till I am dead."——

The keeper interrupted his devotion, by warning him to his fate.—" If there be mercy in you, " replied Henry, " make no noife, for I would not have my dear wife and child awaked till I am no more."

He wept—even he, who was inured to mifery—He, who with apathy had till now looked upon diſtrefs, ſhed tears at Henry's requeſt—Nature, for once predominated in a gaoler.

At this inſtant the child cried ! " O Heavens," said

faid Henry, " I am too guilty to have my prayer heard !" He took up his infant, and fortunately hufhed it again to reft, while the gaoler ftood petrified with grief and aftonifhment. At laft he thus broke out—" This is *too* much, my heart bleeds for you, I would I had not feen this day."—" What do I hear ?" replied Henry. " Is this an angel, in the garb of my keeper ? Thou art indeed unfit for thy office—This is more than I was prepared to hear—Hence, and let me be conducted to my fate.

Thefe words awoke the unhappy Eliza ; who, with eagernefs to atone for loft time, began to appropriate the few moments left, in fupplicating for her hufband's falvation.

Side by fide the unhappy couple prayed, as the Ordinary advanced to the difmal cell—They were too intent on their devotion to obferve him. The holy man came with more comfort than what his function alone could adminifter. It was a *reprieve,* but with caution he communicated the glad tiding to the loving but haplefs pair.

The effect it had on them was too affecting to be exprefled. Henry's fenfes were overpowered, while Eliza became frantic with joy—She ran to the man of God, then to her child, ere fhe perceived her hufband apparently lifelefs. He foon inhaled life, from her tender kiffes, while the humane gaoler gladly knocked off his fetters.——

THE

THE DIFFERENT STAGES OF LIFE

PLEASINGLY DESCRIBED.

HE who, in his YOUTH, improves his *intellectual* powers in the search of truth and useful knowledge ; and refines and strengthens his *moral* and *active* powers by the love of virtue, for the service of his friends, his country, and mankind ; who is animated by true glory, exalted by sacred friendship for *social*, and softened by virtuous love for *domestic* life ; who lays his heart open to every other mild and generous affection, and who to all these adds a sober masculine *piety*, equally remote from *superstition* and *enthusiasm* ; that MAN enjoys the most agreeable *youth* ; and lays in the richest fund for the honourable *action*, and *happy* enjoyment of the *succeeding periods* of life.

HE who, in MANHOOD, keeps the *passions* under due restraint* ; who forms the most select and virtuous friendships ; who seeks after *fame*, *wealth*, and *power*, in the road of *truth* and *virtue* ; and, if he cannot find them in that road, generously despises them ; who in his *private* character and connexions, gives fullest scope to the tender and manly passions ; and in his *public* character and connexions serves his country and mankind, in the most upright and disinterested manner ; who, in fine, enjoys the *goods* of life with
the

---

* The gratifications of vicious passions are always inflamed by enjoyment, and cloy with repetition.

the greateſt *moderation*†, bears its *ills* with Chriſtian *fortitude* ; and in thoſe various circumſtances of *duty* and *trial* maintains and expreſſes an habitual *reverence* and *love of God* ; THAT MAN is the *worthieſt* character in *this ſtage* of life ; paſſes through it with the higheſt ſatisfaction and dignity ; and paves the way to the moſt eaſy and honourable *old age*.

FINALLY, HE, who, in the DECLINE OF LIFE, preſerves himſelf moſt exempt from the chagrins incident to that period ; cheriſhes *kind and benevolent affections* ; uſes his *experience, wiſdom,* and *authority* in the moſt *fatherly* and *venerable* manner ; doing acts under a *ſenſe* of the *inſpection,* and with a view to the *approbation* of his *Maker ;* is conſtantly aſpiring after immortality, and ripening apace for it ; THIS is the *happieſt* OLD-MAN.

Such a truly good man may have ſome enemies, but he will have more friends ; and having given many marks of private friendſhip or public virtue, he can hardly be deſtitute of a patron to protect, or a ſanctuary to entertain him, or to protect or entertain his children when he is gone. Though he ſhould have little elſe to leave them, he bequeaths them the faireſt, and generally the moſt unenvied inheritance of a *good name* ; which, like good ſeed ſown in the field of futurity, will often

M raiſe

† The truly good man is ſatisfied from himſelf, his deſires are moderate, his wants few ; he is cautious without being jealous or diſtruſtful ; careful but not anxious, buſy but not diſtracted ; he taſtes pleaſure without being vicious, and bears pain and affliction without dejection or diſcontent ; is raiſed to power without turning giddy, and feels calamity without repining ; being well aſſured that his heavenly Father will either ſuſtain him under his troubles, or direct and over-rule them for his greateſt good.

raise up unsolicited friends, and yield a benevolent harveft of unexpected charities.

But should the fragrance of the parent's virtue prove offensive to a perverfe or envious age, or even draw down perfecution on the friendlefs orphans ; there is *One* in heaven, who will be more than a father to them, and recompenfe their parent's virtues by showering down blessings on them. The thoughts of leaving them in fuch good hands, fustain the honest parent, and make him smile even in the agonies of death ; being fecure, that that Almighty Friend, who has difpenfed fuch a profufion of bounties to himfelf, cannot prove an unkind guardian, or an unfaithful trustee to his fatherlefs offspring.

ON FLATTERY AND TRUTH.

Stop not to flatter, tho' thou art paid for it.

There is nothing which the majority of the world is more fond of than flattery. This adds inexpreffible delight to weak minds, difplays the moft enticing objects in falfe colours, and too often gains the victory over fincerity and truth. Where it once gains accefs, we foon become enamoured with it, and foolifhly tranfported with its delufive and enfnaring arts. Abfurd indeed ! that men fhould be captivated with fo vain a phantom !

Though flattery may afford us a tranfient pleafure, yet it is as incomparable to truth as light is to darknefs. Experience convinces us that the one cannot

deceive

deceive us, whereas the other is of the moft deceitful nature, acquires a numerous train of apparent
friends, by its enticing delufions, and would, if poffible, gain the predominancy over every individual;
it exhibits every thing delightful to our conception,
and endavours to entangle us by every artifice. But
how different is fincerity or truth ! This ineftimable
quality is truly beneficial to all. He who ufes
this, lives free from perplexing anxiety and folicitude.

His mind is calm and ferene, his heart void of any falfe
imaginations, and he enjoys fcenes of undifturbed repofe. Though flattery may for a time win the affections, yet it is built upon fo ill-grounded a bafis, that
it is always in danger of falling, and being expofed
to public derifion. Whereas truth is blamelefs and
well eftablifhed ; entertains us with a profpect of future tranquility, and makes us ever to abound in the
fruits of folid joy and inward peace.

CHARACTER

OF A

TRUE GENTLEMAN.

A DECENT mein, and elegance of drefs,
Words, which at eafe each winning grace exprefs ;
A life, where love with polifh'd wifdom fhines,
Where wifdom's felf again by love refines ;
Where we to chance for friendfhip never truft,
Nor ever dread from fudden whim, difguft ;
The manners gentle and the heart humane,

A

A nature truly great, but never vain.
A wit, that no licentious pertness knows,
The fenfe, that unaffuming candour fhows;
Reafon, by narrow principles uncheck'd,
Slave to no party, bigot to no fect ;
Knowledge of human life, of learning too,
Thence tafte, and truth, which will from tafte enfue;
A juft difcernment, with a judgment clear,
A fmile indulgent, and that fmile fincere ;
An humble, though an elevated mind,
Its greateft pleafure but to ferve mankind :
Thefe will efteem and admiration raife,
Give true delight, and gain unflattering praife.

GRANDEUR NOT NECESSARY TO
HAPPINESS.

A FRAGMENT.

WHAT true felicity can greatnefs give us, that is
not to be met with in a *middle* ftation of life ? Whoever knows how to limit himfelf to a *moderate* fortune
is truly rich. If a man meafures his neceffities by
nature, he will never be poor ; if by opinion, he will
never be rich. A man need not to be a philofopher
to contemn grandeur, and to know that riches are of
little ufe to the attainment of *true* happinefs.

He need only examine what fuch wealth and grandeur amount to in the end ; for if it be evident to
him that they cannot procure *real* felicity, but are
often pernicious to the owners, he will then be convinced that a ftate of life wherein a perfon has what
is truly neceffary, is far preferable to a ftate of fu-
perfluity and grandeur. . . . .

THE

THE DICTATES OF EXPERIENCE.

THE evils of life, however generally inveighed a-gainft, are moftly of our *own* creating, and to be fur-mounted at pleafure by a little refolution ; the goods of it, fuch as really deferve the name, are within the reach of moft people ; and for the reft, a little Chriftian refignation is an ample *fuccedaneum.* —" How many things are there in this world that I do not want !" faid the philofopher. " How few things are there," replies Folly, " but what I am in abfolute need of !"—*Probatum eft.*

ON MODESTY,

WITH ITS EFFECTS.

MODESTY may juftly be accounted either a virtue or a vice ; or rather, when it is blameable, a foolifh bafhfulnefs ; for then it betrays us into many incon-veniences. How many have been undone becaufe they have not had boldnefs enough to deny the requeft of a *profeffed* friend ! Modefty, in real friendfhip, may be called a vice, when it lets the man we ef-tem run into abfurdities, for fear of difpleafing him by telling him his faults.

In all accidents of life, a man may have too much or too little modefty ; but he that has too much will always fuffer the moft ; foolifh fimplicity hurts itfelf, while daring impudence, in fpite of all oppo-fition, will pufh its way through the world. Eve $\blacktriangleleft$

Ma   what

what is called bafhfulnefs is commended by all, but boldnefs, though it may not have fo much commendation, has more reward : yet, if modefty is not advantageous for profit, it is for virtue ; for it is a thing contradictory in itfelf to fuppofe, that a modeft perfon can be a *wicked* one.

It is certain that many had been, bad that are not, if they had not been bridled by a bafhful nature; for there are many that have hearts for vice who have not a face for it. Modefty, when a virtue, reftrains us from licentious company and bad enterprifes ; it teaches us to efteem merit; it awes the uncivil tongue; prevents a man from vain boafting ; and makes a wife man not to fcorn but to pity a fool.

THE HAPPY MAN.

IN all the different fchemes mankind purfue,
The end's the fame : 'tis *happinefs* in view :
For this, the mariner, while breaking waves
Threat inftant death, the dang'rous paffage brave ;
For this th' aftrologer, whole fleeplefs nights
Fix'd to the tube, explores the ftarry lights ;
For this, the mifer hoards his fhining pelf,
And to be *richly* happy ftarves himfelf ;
For this, fome tread the flipp'ry paths of ftate,
And fancy blifs annex'd to being great ;
Others to diff'rent pleafures give the reins,
While difappointment crowns their fruitlefs pains.
All are deceiv'd who *here* expect to find
Aught that can fatisfy the human mind.
Search thro' the world you'll find ther's nothing can.

Alford.

Afford the proper happpinefs of man, .
That Power alone who gave all beings birth:
Who form'd the heavens, and upholds the earth,
Whofe word firft made, whofe mercy ftill fultains
Thofe worlds unknown, o'er which his juftice reigns,
Whofe fmiles create eternal joy and peace,
Is the true centre of unfading blifs.
   That man alone obtains the end defir'd,
Whofe bofom with immortal love is fir'd ;
Who follows happinefs in virtue's road,
And fteadily obeys the will of God ;
Who will by no temptation be betray'd ;
Nor can by fear of punifhment be fway'd ;
Whofe fixt defign is ftedfaftly purfu'd,
To feek his Maker as his chiefeft good :
Who by God's holy word his way directs,
Watches each word, and every thought infpects ;
Gives up his own to his Creator's mind,
To act, or fuffer, is alike refign'd—
This man (of Heaven's protection ever fure) ,
While thoufands fall around, fhall ftand fecure ;
While thofe who plac'd their happinefs below,
Shall wake from dreams of blifs to endlefs woe.
   He fhall thro' life be happy, and when death,
In gaftly form, demands his fleeting breath,
Th' expected fummons he will gladly hear,
While confcicus virtue diffipates his fear ;
Safely he'll venture thro' the darkfome way,
The deftin'd paffage to eternal day ;
And crown'd with glory which fhall never fade,
Enjoy in heaven that God he here obey'd*.

THE

———×◇◇×———

* Hence learn the real Chriftian is the only happy man
on earth,

THE RURAL VICAR:

A FRAGMENT.

BEING laſt ſummer on a tour to the North, I was one evening arreſted in my progreſs, at the entrance of a ſmall rural hamlet, by breaking the fore wheel of my phæton. This accident rendering it imprac- ticable for me to proceed to the next town, from which I was now *ſixteen* miles diſtant ; I directed my ſteps to a little cottage, at the door of which, in a woodbine arbour ſat a man about *ſixty* years of age, who was ſolacing himſelf with a pipe of tobacco.

In the front of his houſe was affixed a ſmall board which I conceived to contain an intimation, that tra- vellers might there be accommodated. Addreſſing myſelf, therefore, to the old man, I requeſted his aſ- fiſtance, which he readily granted ; but on my men- tioning an intention of remaining at his houſe all night, he regretted that it was not in his power to re- ceive me, and the more ſo, as there was no inn in the village. It was not till now that I diſ- covered my error concerning the board over the door, which contained a notification, that my friend was a ſchoolmaſter, and probably ſecretary to the hamlet.

Affairs were in this ſituation, when the Vicar made his appearance. He was about *ſeventy*, and one of the moſt venerable figures I had ever ſeen ; his time-ſil- vered locks ſhaded his temples, whilſt the lines of misfortune were, alas ! but too viſible in his coun- tenance. Time had in ſome meaſure ſoftened, but could not efface them. On ſeeing my broken equip- age, he addreſſed me ; and when he began to ſpeak, his countenance was illumined by a ſmile. " I pre- ſume, Sir," ſaid he, " that the accident you have
juſt."

juft met with, will render it impoffible for you to proceed. Should that be the cafe, you will be much diftreffed for lodgings, the place affording no accommodation for travellers, as my parifhioners are neither willing nor able to fupport an ale-houfe ; and as we have but few travellers pafs this way, we have little need of one ; but if you will accept the beft accommodation my cottage affords, it is much at your fervice."

After expreffing the grateful fenfe I entertained of his goodnefs, I joyfully accepted fo defirable an offer. As we entered the hamlet, the fun was gilding with his departing beams the village fpire, whilft a gentle breeze refrefhed the weary hinds, who, feated beneath the venerable oaks that overfhadowed their ruftic cottages, were happily repofing themfelves after the fylvan labours of the day.

The Vicar's houfe was fmall, with a thatched roof: the front was entirely covered with woodbines and honey fuckles, which ftrongly fcented the circumambient air. A grove of ancient oaks furrounded the houfe, and preferved the verdure of the adjacent lawn, through the midft of which ran a fmall brook, that gently murmured as it flowed. This, together with the bleating of the fheep, the lowing of the herds, the village murmurs, and the diftant barkings of the trufty curs, who were now entering on their office as guardians of the hamlet, all confpired to entertain the eye, pleafe the ear, and excite the moft agreeable fenfations.

THE

THE

OLD MAN AND HIS DOG.

A PATHETIC NARRATIVE,

TAKEN FROM AN INCIDENT WHICH REALLY

HAPPENED A FEW YEARS AGO.

BEING upon a vifit to a friend near York, as I was one daw walking on the bridge in company with fome ladies, a grey-haired old man came towards us; he fupported himfelf with a ftick; appeared fo lame, that he could fcarcely walk, and was followed by a little terrier. On approaching us, he faid, " Good ladies, will you buy my dog?" The ladies anfwering, that they did not want a dog; he came up to me, and faid in a more prefling manner, and with a more fupplicating tone of voice: " Sir, I befeech you buy my dog!" On my anfwering likewife that I did not want one, the old man remained a few minutes leaning on his ftick; and looking at me with an air of difappointment, feemed to reproach me for declining his requeft, and then uttering a deep figh continued his journey.

As he walked on flowly, before he was out of fight, Louifa, one of the young ladies, whifpered me, " Pray Sir, go after him, and buy his dog, for the poor man feems in diftrefs." I accordingly called the old man back, and afked him what was the price of the dog? " What you pleafe," he returned. " Here is a *crown*," I replied; " if that will fatisfy you, take it, and leave me your dog."—" The dog is yours," faid the old man, " and God blefs you with it."—" But," faid I, " he will never follow me, how fhall I prevent

-vent his efcape ?"—" True" replied the old man, "he'
muft be tied, or he will follow *me*." He then untied
his garter, called " *Trim*," took him up in his arms,
and placed him upon the parapet of the bridge ;
while he was faftening the garter round his neck, I
perceived the hands of the old man trembling, which
I imputed to his age ; for his countenance did not
change. Having faftened the knot, he inclined his
head towards the dog, and fixing his mouth upon
his body, remained for a few minutes in that pofture
motionlefs and without uttering a fingle word. I
approached him, and faid, " Friend, what is the
matter ?"—" Nothing," he anfwered, " but what
will foon be forgotten !" and I obferved his cheek
wet with tears. " You feem," faid I, " to regret
parting with your dog."—" Alas ! it is truly fo ;
he is the only friend I have ⬛ e world ; we have
never been feparated from each other. He was my
guard on the road when I was afleep ; and whenever he faw me fatigued and fuffering, the poor creature licked my face, and feemed to cafe my pain
with his careffes ; he loves me fo much, that it is
but natural I fhould love him in return. But all
this is nothing to you, he is now yours :" and he offered me the garter which he had juft faftened
round his neck.

"You muft have a very bad opinion of me," faid I,
" if you think that I am capable of depriving you
of a faithful friend, and the only friend you have
in the world." He feemed affected and offered to
return the crown ; but I told him to keep the money and the dog too. Before I could prevent him,
the old man threw himfelf upon his knees, and exclaimed, " Good Sir, I owe you my life ; hunger
had reduced me to the moft extreme neceffity."——
These expreffions urged my curiofity ; and leading

ing him from one queſtion to another, I collected the
following account : " Thank heaven," he ſaid, " I
have lived *fifty* years by the labour of my hands, and
yeſterday, for the firſt time in my life, I aſked charity. I am by trade a carpenter, and was ſettled at
Catterick, till on chopping a piece of wood, I cut
my leg with an axe, and have been ſince incapable
of working. I am now going to Sheffield, where I
have a ſon, who is employed in the manufactures,
and who will not let me want 'for any thing. But
as the journey is long, and I can ſcarcely drag myſelf along on account of my wound, I have ſpent
the little money which I had been able to ſave, and
am obliged to beg for ſuſtenance : though, as I do
not look poor, I got but little ; and being exhauſted
with hunger, I had nothing but my poor dog."

Here his voice failed him ; and his ſobs prevented
him from continuing. " At your age," I replied,
" and in this hot weather, and with a bad leg, I cannot ſuffer you to continue ſo long a journey on foot ;
you will inflame your wound, and render it incura-
ble. Follow me ; Providence here offers you an
aſylum; where you will find reſt, affiſtance, and perhaps a cure." The old man ſaid nothing, but unty-
ing his dog, followed me to the infirmary. Fortunately the ſurgeon happened to be in the houſe, and
on mentioning the poor man's ſituation, he immediately looked at the wound, which was highly inflamed with the heat of the weather, and the fatigue
of the journey. " It is fortunate," ſaid the ſurgeon,
" that he did not continue his journey a few hours
later, as he muſt have loſt his leg, but I can now
cure it."—" He will then get well ?" ſaid I. " Yes,"
replied the ſurgeon ; " I will anſwer for the cure,
provided he will continue perfectly quiet."

As he was going up ſtairs, followed by his faithful

-ful terrier, the porter laid hold of *Trim*, and was preparing to carry him out of the houſe. " *Trim*," ſaid, the old man, " may not poor *Trim* follow me ?"—" It is againſt the rules of the houſe," returned the matron, " to admit any dogs into the wards." —" Alas," replied the old man, " *Trim* will not be happy if he is not with me, and I ſhall not be happy if he is unhappy."—" It is a pity to part good, friends," exclaimed the ſurgeon ; " I am convinced that my patient will ſoon get well, if Trim and he are not parted." Then, turning to the matron, " For once," he ſaid, " let us break through the rules of the houſe. If *Trim* behaves well, let him ſtay by his maſter's bed."—" I will anſwer," returned the old man, " for *Trim's* behaviour ; he will lie by me whole hours without ſtirring from his ſituation, and if he may be ſuffered to follow me, I am ſure he will be as quiet as a mouſe."

Theſe words intereſted every one in favour of *Trim* ; the porter inſtantly ſet him down, *Trim* bounded up ſtairs with great agility, and as if aware of what had paſſed, fawned upon the ſurgeon, and then quietly followed his maſter.

Having thus left the old man and his dog in ſuch good hands, I returned to the company, and related all that had paſſed : all pitied the poor man, and rejoiced at the hopes of his recovery; but Louiſa firſt put half a guinea into my hands ; the remainder of the company followed her example, ſome gave more and ſome leſs ; and I undertook to be the old man's treaſurer.

Meanwhile the ſtory circulated, and every one wiſhed to hear the tale of the *Old Man and his Dog Trim*. In repeating it I particularly dwelt upon the crown which I offered for the dog, and ſeveral ironically admired the exceſs of my generoſity.

N   Louiſa

Louisa would say, " Only a *crown* for so inestimable
a dog !" and her opinion was sure to be adopted by
the generality of the company. " And you, Sir,"
I would say, " and you, Madam, how much would
you have given ?" Each person mentioned the sum
which they would have contributed, augmenting or
diminishing it according to the sensibility of their
hearts ; or the impression which the recital had made
upon them.. " Well," I replied, " the old man is
not far from hence, and you may now contribute
what you would have given in my place."

By these means their charity was excited by emu-
lation ; a comfortable sum was obtained ; the old
man recovered, and I conducted him to the man-
sion-house, almost as lively and as frisky as his
dog. Both were received with general satisfaction,
poor *Trim* was the most taken notice of : in his life
he never received so many caresses, and from none
more than from the charming Louisa. *Trim* was at
first confounded, but he soon appeared as if he knew
why he was so much caressed. The old man dined
and supped in the servants' hall, with *Trim* by his
side.

The next morning, he came to take leave of me ;
I put into his hands the collection that had been
made for him ; and in vain I assured him that I
had contributed nothing. " I can never forget,"
exclaimed he, " that I owe you every thing :" in
saying these words he endeavoured to throw himself at my feet ; in struggling to prevent him, he
threw himself into my arms, and we embraced and
bid adieu to each other, as if we had been old
friends. " Sir," said he, " you have loaded me
with favours, but I shall ask of you another favour ;
you have embraced me, will you condescend to kiss
Trim ? I shall be happy to acquaint my son that
you

you have kiffed my dog. Come, *Trim* come, the gntleman will do you the honour to carefs you." *Trim* rofe upon his hind legs, and pawed me with his fore feet as I ftooped down to pat him ; and as I inclined my head, the figure of the old man inclining his head on the dog as I was then doing, and thinking that he was embracing him for the laft time, prefented itfelf fo forcibly to my imagination, that the tears ftarted from my eyes. " Ah !" exclaimed the old man, " ah ! you love *Trim*, I fee ; keep him ; he is ftill your's." " No, my good friend," I replied, " go, and the blefling of God attend you. I now feel myfelf happier than I deferve, and be affured that the image of you and your dog will never be effaced from my recollection."

At this moment Louifa entered the room with a plate of meat for the dog. She fet it down before him, and while *Trim* was feeding, fhe tied round his neck a rofe-coloured ribband. I faid to the old man, " There is the perfon to whom your thanks are due ; without her I fhould never have bought your dog ; without her you would never have been cured ; and without her your little favourite *Trim* would not have been decorated with this rofe-coloured collar." The old man, inftantly taking up his dog, placed it in Louifa's arms. " *Trim*, here is your miftrefs : this, madam, is the only recompence in my power to make for your kind favours ;" and feeing the dog ftruggling to get loofe, he added, " *Trim* is not fond of ftrangers, but foon becomes attached to thofe he knows, and who are kind to him. He is not handfome, but he is a good creature. I am happy in procuring for him a kind and affectionate miftrefs." So faying, he drew his hand acrofs his eyes, and quitted the door. Louifa, holding the dog in her arms, continued ftroking and careffing it ; but when the creature

creature, inftead of returning her careffes, ftruggled to get loofe, fhe opened the houfe-door, and putting the dog upon the ground, *Trim* immediately ran after his mafter, and foon overtook him. The old man ftoped, took him up in his arms, and preffed him to his bofom ; then taking off his hat, and waving it as a token of fatisfaction and gratitude, haftened his pace, and in a few minutes both he and *Trim* were out of fight.

THE WHISTLE,

BY DOCTOR FRANKLIN :-

A TRUE STORY,

WRITTEN TO HIS NEPHEW.

WHEN I was a child, about feven years old, my friends, on a holiday, filled my pocket with halfpence. I went directly to a fhop where they fold toys for children ; but being charmed with the found of the whiftle, that I met with by the way in the hands of another boy, I voluntarily offered him all my money for it. I then came home, and went whiftling all over the houfe, much pleafed with my whiftle, but difturbing all the family. My brothers and fifters, and coufins, underftanding the bargain I had made, told me I had given four times as much for it as it was worth. This put me in mind of what good things I might have bought with
the

the reft of the money; and they laughed at me fo much for my folly, that I cried with vexation ; and the reflection gave me more chagrin than the whiftle gave me pleafure.

This however was afterwards of ufe to me, the impreffion continuing on my mind, fo that often, when I was tempted to buy fome unneceffary thing, I faid to myfelf, " Do not give too much for the *whif-tle* ;" and fo I faved my money.

As I grew up, came into the world, and obferved the actions of men, I thought I met with many, very many, who " gave too much for the whiftle."

When I faw any one ambitious of court favours, facrificing his time in attendance on levees ; his repofe, his liberty, his virtue, and perhaps his friends, to attain it, I have faid to myfelf, " This man gives too much for his whiftle*."

When I faw another fond of popularity, conftantly employing himfelf in political buftles, neglecting his own affairs, and ruining them by that neglect; " He pays, indeed," fays I, " too much for his whiftle."

If I knew a mifer, who gave up every kind of comfortable living, all the pleafure of doing good to others, all the efteem of his fellow-citizens, and the joys of benevolent friendfhip, for the fake of accumulating wealth : " Poor man," fays I, " you do indeed pay too much for your whiftle."

N 2   When

---

* If you wifh to be happy, be not fond of honours, ambitious of power, covetous of riches, or a flave to pleafure.

When I meet a man of pleasure, sacrificing every laudable improvement of the mind, or of his fortune, to mere corporeal sensations; " Mistaken man," says I, " you are providing pain for yourself, instead of pleasure : you give too much for your whistle."

If I see one fond of fine clothes, fine furniture, fine equipages, all above his fortune, for which he contracts debts, and ends his career in a prison; " Alas," says I, " he has paid dear, *very* dear for his whistle."

When I see a beautiful, sweet-tempered girl, married to an ill-natured brute of a husband : " What a pity it is," says I, " that she has paid so much for a whistle !"

In short, I conceived that great part of the miseries of mankind were brought upon them, by the false estimate they had made of the value of things, and by their giving too much for their *whistles.*

THE

THE BENEFITS

OF

WISDOM AND REPUTATION,

IN THE COMMON AFFAIRS OF HUMAN LIFE.

IT is a juft obfervation of a great man, that a-mong all the complaints which are generally made for want of the good things of life, no man ever complains for want of *wifdom*.—People will readily enough allow that others excel them in perfon, for-tune, rank, or learning ; and will even think it a hardfhip that they have not received fo plentiful a distribution of thofe things as their neighbours ; but, as to *wifdom* (or a prudent management of ourfelves in worldly affairs), every man fits down fully contented with his own fhare ; and is fo far from envy-ing his neighbour's excellence, that he rather pities or defpifes him for want of that ample portion which he thinks has been adminiftered to himfelf.

Our conduct may be confidered in the general, as refpecting ourfelves, and our fellow-creatures ; by the firft we confult our private eafe and convenience; by the fecond, our public character, or reputation ; which conftitute the fum and fubftance of the good things of life.

A man who takes care to preferve a general good character, will hardly fail of compaffing his ends fome time or other. On the contrary, an ill name hangs over a man like the naked fword over the head of Damocles, and he can never be fecure that it will not fall upon him. There are, indeed, inftances of men, who by (what is generally ftyled) a good hit

in

in bufinefs, or by the aid of a great fortune, go on
and flourifh in the world, though every one that
knows them, both fpeaks and thinks ill of them ;
and of others, who are univerfally efteemed and commended for their diligence and affability, and yet
unfuccefsful intheir attempts and defigns* ; but thefe
perfons muft be ftyled exceptions to a general rule.

Sincerity and punctuality are two qualities that add
a wonderful luftre to our reputation among our
neighbours and acquaintance. ' It will oftentimes
coft a man very great trouble, and bring him to
many inconveniences, to keep up thofe characters;
but be the pains ever fo gerat, the reward is anfwer-
able.

If a man fhould hear himfelf blamed for any
proceedings in his conduct relating to his private affairs, he may poffibly have good reafon to comfort
himfelf with the belief, that thofe who cenfure him,
on this account, are miftaken. But if he finds
himfelf difliked for any defect in his outward behaviour, fuch as for being *ill-natured, morofe, affected,
conceited*, or any fuch faults as may render him difagreeable or ridiculous, he has a great deal of reafon to attend to fuch reflections, and carefully to examine his conduct by them, in order to reform himfelf; becaufe fuch things come very properly under
the cognizance of thofe we have to do with : and,
inftead of being offended, as men are very apt to
be upon fuch occafions, every one ought to treafure up fuch animadverfions with great care ; and
look upon them as choice admonitions, and ufeful
rules, to direct their behaviour by for the future.

TRUE.

---

* The race is not always to the fwift, nor the battle to
the ftrong ; fuccefs is only of the Lord, who is the rewar-
der of all thofe whe diligently feek him.

TRUE HAPPINESS:

AN ESSAY.

WHOEVER neglects to reflect how happy he is, in order to confider how much happier he might be, by comparing, his own fituation with that of others, ingenioufly contrives to torment himfelf, and opens a perpetual fource of mifery and difcontent. He will never be at peace, fince it is impoffible for riches, beauty, ftrength, wifdom, power, and every other bleffing, to centre in *one* man ; and, in truth, if fuch an union were poffible, he would ftill remain in the fame unhappy fituation ; as the dif-quietude of his temper would lead him to reflect, that he ftill wanted many qualities inherent in other animals ; and would perhaps point out to him a fubject for envy, even in a *lion*, or a *butterfly*.

Man would be a much happier being if he did not fo induftrioufly endeavour to draw misfortunes and calamities upon himfelf.

The greateft curfe that heaven can entail on men, is to leave them entirely to themfelves, to gratify all their idle wifhes and defires. They do not forefee the confequences of the things they afk for. When they wifh for pleafure, they do not think of difeafe and death ; and when they defire wealth or honour, they forget the fnares and temptations which attend the poffeffion of them.

The loweft fituation in life has its peculiar com-forts and conveniences, and if it fhares not in the fplendour

dour of profperity, it is alfo free from its numerous folicitudes*.

Happinefs is perhaps more equally diftributed than is generally imagined ; and whoever is dif-appointed in his views of elevation and great-nefs, is fheltered likewife from the cares und anx-ieties, which attend the rich, and protected from the envy and malevolence that wait on the am-bitious.

Every ftation has its inconveniencies, and it is bet-ter to bear with thofe we are accuftomed to endure, and of which we know the utmoft extent, than by aiming at the feeming advantages of another way of life, to fubject ourfelves alfo to its miferies, which may perhaps be greater than thofe we groan under at prefent.

> Wifh not for wealth, nor grandeur prize ;
> True happinefs in *Contentment* lies.

THE BENEFITS

OF

CONTENTMENT.

ADDRESSED TO A YOUNG GENTLEMAN.

LET your moft fervent and daily prayers to heaven be directed for the greateft bleffings of human life, the bleffings of *virtue* and *content*. How foon my dear young

---

* Tho' hardfhips may the poor purfue,
The rich have cares and troubles too.   W.

young friend, will a right fenfe of what is really a fufficiency teach you to fmile at the boundlefs defires of ambition, the idle pomp of greatnefs, and the fuperfluous wants of an inordinate fancy ! if you can but once have that command over your paffions, either for *drefs*, *diverfions*, or all the *et ceteras* in the catalogue of juvenile defires, as to fay unto them, " Thus far fhall ye go, and no farther ;" then will you acquire all that is moft to be defired ; a ferenity undifturbed by imaginary wants, a peace, which paffeth all the tumults of fortune and giddinefs of gaiety : a philofophy built upon the foul's conviction, and ftrengthened by the ennobling fentiments of Chriftianity.

THE

PLEASURES AND PURSUITS

OF

HUMAN LIFE.

AN ESSAY.

" O with what joy would I refign my breath !
The Wretch exclaims, and prays for inftant death ;
The fiend approaching, he inverts his pray'r,
O grant me life, and double all my care !"

Man is continually complaining of the cares and miferies of life, and yet dreading nothing fo much as the approach of death to his relief. A wife and good man knows, that care muft be more or lefs his portion in this life, and that it is his duty to endure it with patience and refignation. Labour, poverty,
                                                                and

and difeafes, with numberlefs difappointments in
our feveral purfuits, muft be expected and fuftained ;
and he is the beft and happieft man, who neither wifhes for the approach of death, nor is afraid to
meet it*.

There is an analogy between the circumftances of
the higheft and the loweft among mankind, which
is very much calculated to flatter that pride and vanity fo incident to human nature. The fame parts
are acted, but in a different fphere, by a circle of
courtiers and a company of beggars.

One man is perhaps the wonder of all the known
world, another is the admiration of a particular country, another is the pride of a great city, and another
is the firft character in a village. All thefe fhine il-
luftrioufly, and with proper dignity and fplendour in
their feveral orbs : but fhuffle them out of their fta-
tions, place the villager at the head of an immenfe
army, and confine the hero within the boundaries of
a little town, perhaps they would both appear ridiculous.

The laugh however will always run ftrongeft a-
gainft *him*, that elevates himfelf to a dignity which
he cannot fupport ; and though he might be ap-
plauded within his own narrow circle, when he comes
on the grand theatre of the world, he cannot fail to
be univerfally derided.

The mind of man is not formed for unremitted attention, nor his body for uninterrupted labour ; and
we can no more go through any bufinefs requiring
intenfe thought, without unbending the mind, and
relaxing it from the fatigue of contemplation,
than

---

* Nothing can accomplifh this, but the dictates of religion.

than we can perform a long journey without refreſhing ourſelves by due reſt at the ſeveral ſtages of it. The faculties, always kept on the ſtretch, loſe their tone and vigour, and become dull and languid. The mind is formed for contemplation, the body for exerciſe; but continual labour would deſtroy both. We ſhould not therefore be aſhamed to relax at proper intervals; and as the Sabbath renews the ſtrength of the peaſants, and fits them to return to their labours with freſh cheerfulneſs; ſo a little holiday in our ſtudies qualifies us to purſue them with freſh aſſiduity, and greater probability of ſucceſs.

> Meditate, but ſlight not labour;
> Labour, but ſlight not meditation.

ſCHEMES OF LIFE DEFEATED BY IRRESOLUTION.

AN EASTERN TALE.

OMAR, the ſon of Haſſan, had paſſed ſeventy-five years in honour and proſperity. The favour of three ſucceſſive Califfs had filled his houſe with riches, and whenever he appeared, the benedictions of the people proclaimed his approach.

Terreſtrial happineſs is of ſhort continuance. The brightneſs of the flame is waſting its fuel, and the fragrant flower paſſing away in its own odours. The vigour of Omar began to fail, the curls of beauty fell from his head, ſtrength departed from his hands, and agility from his feet. He gave back to the Califf the keys of truſt and the ſeals of ſecrecy; and ſought no other pleaſure for the re

O   mainder

mainder of his days, than the converfe of the
wife, and the gratitude of the poor whom he relieved.

The powers of his mind were yet unimpaired.
His chamber was filled by vifitants, eager to catch
the dictates of experience, and officious to pay the
tribute of admiration. Caled, the fon of the viceroy
of Egypt, entered every day early, and retired late:
he was beautiful and eloquent ; Omar admired his
wit, and loved his docility. "Tell me," faid Caled,
"thou to whofe voice nations have liftened with admiration and whofe wifdom is known to the ex-
tremities of Afia, tell me how I may refemble Omar
the prudent. The arts by which thou haft gained
power and preferved it, are no longer neceffary or
ufeful to thee ; impart to me therefore the fecret of
thy conduct, and teach me the plan on which thy
wifdom has built thy fame.

"Young man," faid Omar, "it is of little ufe to
form plans of life. When I took my firft furvey of
the world, in my twentieth year, having confidered
the various conditions of mankind, in the hour of
folitude I faid thus to myfelf, leaning againft a
cedar which fpread its branches over my head—Sev-
enty years are allowed to man ; I have yet fifty remaining : ten years I will allot to the attainment of
knowledge, and ten I will pafs in foreign countries ;
I fhall be learned, and confequently fhall be honoured ; every city will fhout at my arrival, and
every ftudent will folicit my acquaintance. Twenty years thus paffed will ftore my mind with images,
which I fhall be bufy through the reft of my life
in combining and comparing. I fhall revel in frefh
accumulations of intellectual wealth, I fhall find
new pleafures for every moment, and fhall never
more be weary of myfelf.

"I will

" I will, however, not deviate too far from the beaten track of common life, but will try what can be found in *female* converfation. I will marry a wife beatiful as the Houries, and wife as Zobeide ; with her I will live twenty years within the fub-urbs of Bagdat, in every pleafure that wealth can purchafe, and fancy can invent. I will then retire to a rural dwelling, pafs my laft days in obfcurity and contemplation ; and lie filently down on the bed of death. Through my life it fhall be my fettled refolution, never to depend on the fmiles of princes ; nor ftand expofed to the artifices of courts ; I will never pant for public honours, nor difturb my quiet with affairs of ftate. Such was my fcheme of life in my *younger* days.

" The firft part of my enfuing time was to be fpent in fearch of knowledge, and I know not how I was diverted from my defign. I had no vifible impediments without, nor fuffered any ungovern-able paffions within. I regarded knowledge as the higheft honour and moft engaging pleafure ; yet day ftole on day, and mouth glided after mouth, till I found that *feven* years of the firft ten had vanifhed, and left nothing behind them. I now poftponed my purpofe of travelling ; for why fhould I go abroad while fo much remained to be learned at home ? I therefore immured myfelf at home for *four* years, and ftudied the laws of the empire. The fame of my knowledge reached even the judges ; I was found able to fpeak upon doubt-ful queftions, and was commanded to ftand at the footftool of the fupreme Califf. I was heard with attention, I was confulted with confidence, and the love of praife faftened on my heart.

" I ftill wifhed to fee diftant countries, liftened with rapture to the relations of travellers, and resolved

refolved to afk my difmiffion, that I might feaft
my foul with novelty ; but my prefence was always
neceffary, and the ftream of bufinefs hurried me
along. Sometimes I was afraid left I fhould be
charged with ingratitude ; but I propofed to travel,
and therefore would not confine myfelf by marriage.

"In my *fiftieth* year I began to fufpect that the
time of travelling was paft, and thought it beft to
lay hold on the felicity yet in my power, and indulge myfelf in *domeftic* pleafures. But at fifty
no man eafily finds a woman beautiful as the Houries, and wife as Zobeide. I inquired and rejected,
confulted and deliberated ; till the *fixty-fecond* year
made me afhamed of gazing upon girls. I had
now nothing left but retirement, and for retirement
I never found a time, till difeafe forced me from
public employment.————

"Such was my fcheme, and fuch has been its
confequences. With an infatiable thirft for knowledge, I trifled away the years of improvement ;
with a reftlefs defire of feeing different countries,
I have always refided in the fame city ; with the
higheft expectation of connubial felicity, I have lived
unmarried ; and with unalterable refolutions of
contemplative retirement, I am going to die within
the walls of Bagdat."————

———◄◎►———

AN
OLD MAN'S ADDRESS TO YOUTH.
BY THE LATE JONAS HANWAY, ESQ.
———

Let none on *future* time rely,
For none can be too young to die.   W.

YOU will not be furprifed that I fhould *preach ;*
I am defcending into the vale of years ; *you* are going

ing up the hill, to take a view of what I have often feen. Many a long day have I beheld the vanities of of the world. Many of the faults of others are obvious to me ; and fo are fome of my own. Things wear a different afpect in your eyes : If I now officioufly intrude on your gayer hours, I remind you that it is not always *fpring* nor *fummer*.

You expect in due time to reach the *winter* of your days ; and what do you imagine will *then* contribute moft to your comfort, and brighten your profpect beyond the grave ? You have my fincereft wifhes that your hopes may always bloffom in the fulleft charms of vernal beauty, till in the great progrefs of human wifdom, your paffions being lulled to reft, your enjoyments may become pure as the limpid ftream, bright as the meridian fun, and calm as a fummer fea. Some degree of forrow is the lot of every mortal ; but I truft that *your profperity* will never be impaired by the want of virtue, nor your *adverfity* be devoid of folid confolation.

Ere long you muft deliver up your material part to be the fport of elements ; but as Nature in her yearly courfe, reftores the beauty of the *faireft flowers*, though appearing irrevocably loft, your frame being diffolved, will again unite with your angelic fpirit ; and both together I hope, be made perfectly happy in the realms of everlafting blifs and glory,

Tho' age *muft* die, youth alfo *may*,
O then prepare without delay, }
For death and for the judgment day. W.

REFLECTIONS

ON THE

BEING AND PROVIDENCE OF GOD.

WHEREVER right conceptions of God and his providence prevail, when he is confidered as the inexhaufted fource of light, love, and joy ; as acting in the joint characters of a *father* and *governor*, imparting an endlefs variety of capacities to his creatures, and fupplying them with every thing neceffary to their full completion and happinefs ; what veneration and gratitude muft fuch conceptions, thoroughly believed, excite in the human mind ? How natural and delightful muft it be to one whofe heart is open to the perception of truth, and of every thing *fair*, *great*, and *wonderful* in nature, to comtemplate and adore him, who is the firft *fair*, the firft *great*, and firft *wonderful :* in whom *wifdom, power,* and *goodnefs* dwell vitally, effentially, originally, and act in perfect concert ? What *grandeur* is here to fill the moft enlarged capacity ! what *beauty* to engage the moft ardent love ! what a mafs of *wonders* in fuch exuberance of perfection, to aftonifh and delight the foul of man through an eternal duration !

If the *Deity* is confidered as our fupreme *guardian* and *benefactor ;* as the *Father of Mercies,* who loves his creatures with infinite tendernefs, and, in a particular manner, all *good* men, nay, all who delight in goodnefs even in its moft imperfect degrees ; what refignation, what dependance, what generous confidence, what hope in God and his all-wife Providence, muft arife in the foul that is poffeffed of fuch amia-

ble

ble views of him ? All thofe exercifes of piety, and above all a fuperlative efteem and love, are directed to God as to their *natural*, their *ultimate*, and indeed their only *adequate* object*; and though the immenfe obligations we are under to him, for all the benefits he hath beftowed upon us, may excite more lively feelings of divine goodnefs, than a general and abftracted contemplation of it ; yet the affections of *gratitude* and *love* are of themfelves of the generous, difinterefted kind, not the refult of felf-intereft, or views of reward.

A perfect character, in which we always fuppofe infinite goodnefs, guided by unerring wifdom, and fupported by almighty power, is the only proper object of perfect and univerfal love. Whoever indulges fuch noble and juft fentiments and affections towards the great Creator, muft be confirmed in the love of virtue ; in a defire to imitate its all-perfect Pattern ; and in a cheerful fecurity and confidence that all his moft important concerns, as well as thofe of his friends and of the univerfe at large fhall be abfolutely fafe under the conduct of his unerring wifdom and unbounded goodnefs. It is in his care and providence alone, that the good man, who is anxious for the happinefs of all, finds perfect ferenity ; a ferenity neither ruffled by partial ill, not foured by private difappointment.   FORDYCE.

THE

---

* The duties we owe to God, as our Creator, Preferver, and daily benefactor, are reverence, gratitude, love, obedience, refignation, dependance, worfhip, and praife.

THE

SUBLIME NATURE AND ADVANTAGES

OF

RELIGION.

Religion ! thou the foul of happinefs !

NIGHT THOUGHTS.

RELIGION is the daughter of Heaven, parent of our virtues, and fource of all true felicity ; fhe alone giveth peace and contentment, divefts the heart of anxious cares, burfts on the mind a flood of joy, and fheds unmingled and perpetual funfhine in the pious breaft. By her the fpirits of darknefs are banifhed from the earth, and angelic minifters of grace thicken unfeen the regions of mortality. She promotes love and good-will among men, lifts up the head that hangs down, heals the wounded fpirit, diffipates the gloom of forrow, fweetens the cup of affliction, blunts the fting of death, and wherever feen, felt, and enjoyed, breathes around her an everlafting fpring. Religion raifes men above themfelves ; irreligion finks them beneath the brutes ; the one makes them angels, the other makes them devils ; *this* binds them down to a poor pitiable fpeck of perifhable earth ; *that* opens up a vifta to the fkies, and lets loofe all the principles of an immortal mind, among the glorious objects of an eternal world.

Lift up thy head, O Chriftian ! and look foward to yon calm unclouded regions of mercy, unfullied by vapours,

vapours, unruffled by ftorms ; where celeftial friendfhip, the lovelieft form in heaven, never dies,
never changes, never cools !' Ere long thou
fhalt burft this brittle earthly prifón of the body, break
through the fetters of mortality, fpring to endlefs
life, and mingle with the fkies. Corruption has but
a limited duration. Happinefs is even now in the
bud : a few days, weeks, or *years* at moft, and that
bud fhall be fully blown. Here virtue droops under
a thoufand preffures ; but, like the earth with the returning fpring, fhall then renew her youth, renew her
verdure, and rife and reign in never-fading and undi-
minifhed luftre. It does not fignify what thy profpects now are ; or what thy fituation now is. In the
prefent world thy heart, indeed, may fob and bleed
its laft, before thou fhalt meet with one, who has either the generofity to relieve, or the humanity to pity thee. Thou haft, however, in the compaffionate
Parent of creation, a moft certain refource in the
deepeft extremity. Caft thine eyes but a little beyond this ftrange, myfterious, and perplexing fcene,·
which at prefent intercepts thy views of futurity. Behold a bow ftamped in the darkeft cloud that lowers
in the face of heaven, and the whole furrounding hemifphere brightening as thou approacheft !
Say, does not yon bleffed opening, which overlcoks
the dark dominion of the grave, more than compen-
fate all the fighs and fufferings, which chequer the
prefent, intervening fcene ? Lo ! there thy long-loft
friend, who ftill lives in thy remembrance, whofe prefence gave thee more delight than all that life could
afford, and whofe abfence coft thee more groans and
tears than all that death can take away—beckons
thee to him, that where he is thou mayeft be
alfo. " Here," he fays, " dwell unmingled pleafures, unpolluted joys, inextinguifhable love, immortal,

tal, unbounded, and unmolested friendship. All the sorrows and imperfections of mortality are to us as though they had never been ; and nothing lives in heaven, but pure unadulterated devotion. Our hearts, swelled with rapture, ceafe to murmur ; our breasts, warm with gratitude, ceafe to figh ; our eyes, charmed with celeftial visions, to shed tears ; our hands, enriched with palms of victory, to tremble ; and our heads, encircled with glory, to ache. We are just as safe as infinite power, as joyful as infinite fulness, and as happy as infinite goodness, can make us. Ours is peace without moleftation, plenty without want, health without fickness, day without night, pleasure without pain, and life without the least mixture or dread of diffolution."

Happy thou, to whom the prefent life has no charm, for which thou canft wifh it to be protracted ! Thy troubles will foon vanish like a dream, which mocks the power of memory ; and what fignify all the fhocks which thy delicate and feeling fpirit can meet with in this tranfitory world ? A few moments longer, and thy complaints will be for ever at an end ; thy difeafes of body and mind fhall be felt no more ; the ungenerous hints of churlish relations fhall diftrefs, fortune frown, and futurity intimidate, no more. Then fhall thy voice, no longer breathing the plaintive ftrains of melancholy, but happily attuned to fongs of gladnefs, mingle with the hofts of heaven, in the laft and fweeteft anthem that ever mortals or immortal fung, " O Death ! where is thy fting ? O Grave ! where is thy victory ?— Thanks be to God, who giveth us the victory through our Lord Jefus Chrift ;—Bleffing and honour, glory and power, be unto Him that fits on the throne, and unto the Lamb, for ever and ever."

THE

ADDRESS OF A SKELETON,

TO

MANKIND IN GENERAL,

AND WELL DESERVING THE REGARD OF ALL.

WHY ſtart ? the caſe is yours, or will be ſoon,
Some *years* perhaps, perhaps another moon ;
Life at its utmoſt ſpan is but a breath,
And they who longeſt dream muſt wake at death*.
Like you I once thought every bliſs ſecure,
And gold, of every ill the certain cure ;
Till ſteep'd in ſorrow and beſieg'd with pain,
Too late I found all earthly riches vain.
Diſeaſe with ſcorn threw back the ſordid fee,
And Death too anſwer'd, " What is gold to me ?"
Fame, titles, honours, theſe I vainly ſought,
And fools obſequious nurs'd the childiſh thought ;
Circled with brib'd applauſe and purchas'd praiſe,
I built on endleſs raptures endleſs days ;
Till death awak'd me from my dream of pride,
And laid a prouder beggar by my ſide.

Pleaſure

---

* O ye ſons and daughters of mortality ! ye candidates of
pleaſure and votaries of diſſipation, whether young or old,
rich or poor, noble or unknown ! remember, in the midſt of
life ye are in death ; ere another morning ye may be ſum-
moned to appear before God in judgment---and what think
ye will be your final and everlaſting doom !

Pleasure I courted, and obey'd my taste,
While every day did yield some new repast;
A loathsome carcase was my constant care,
And worlds were ransack'd but for me to share.
 Go on, vain man? to luxury be firm,
But know thou feastest but to feast a *worm*[*].
Farewell ; remember, nor my words despise,
The only happy are the early wise.

THE

CHOICE AND CRITERION

OF

TRUE PIETY.

Search the Scriptures.

WOULD you wish, amidst the great variety of religious systems in vogue, to make a right distinction,
and prefer the *best*? Recollect the character of Christ;
keep a steady eye on that universal and permanent
good-will to men, in which he lived, by which he suf-
fered, and for which he died.   What now would you
expect from a mind so purely and habitually benign?
Is it possible to suppose, that a heart thus warm and
wide could harbour a narrow wish, or utter a partial sentiment ? Most luckily, in this point the fullest
                                   satisfaction

---

[*] Job, xxv. 6. Psalm, xxii. 6.

fatisfaction is in every man's power. Go, fearch the religion he has left, to the bottom, not in thofe artificial theories, which have done it the moft effential injury ; nor in their manner who affume his name, but overlook his example, and who are talking for ever about the merits of his death, at the expence of. thofe virtues which adorned his life ; not in thofe wild and romantic opinions, which, to make us Chriftians, would make us fools : but in thofe infpir-ed writings, and in thofe alone, which contain his genuine hiftory and his bleffed gofpel ; and which, in the moft peculiar and exclufive fenfe, are the words of eternal life.

Read the Scriptures then as you would the LAST WILL of fome deceafed friend, in which you expected a large bequeft ; and tell me, in the fincerity of your foul, what you fee there to circumfcribe the focial affections, to quafh the rifings of benevolence, or to check the generous effufions of humanity. Littlenefs of mind and narrownefs of temper were certainly no parts of our Saviour's character ; and he enjoins nothing which he did not himfelf uniformly and minutely exemplify. Strange ! that an inftitution, which begins and ends in benignity, fhould be proftituted to countenance the workings of malevolent paffions, fhould produce animofities among thofe whom it was intended to unite ! But there is not a corruption in the humane heart which has not fometimes borrowed the garb of religion. Chriftianity, however is not the lefs precious to the honeft, becaufe knaves and hypocrites have fo long abufed her ; and, let bigots and fceptics fay what they pleafe, fhe foftens and enlarges the heart, warms and impregnates the mind of man, as certainly, and as fenfibly, as the fun does the earth.

P   This

'This CRITERION is as obvious as it is decifive. True
humility and benevolence are always acceptable, and
always known.   Whoever would be thought pious,
without thefe genuine fignatures of piety ; be his behaviour as ftarch,and his face as fad and fanctimonious
as he will, mark him down for nothing but a *hypocrite.*
He alone whofe bofom fwells with the milk of human
kindnefs, who would not fay or do any thing to hurt
another for a world ; whofe daily aim and difpofition is to live foberly, righteoufly, and godly, whatever fyftem he may adopt, lives under the vifible influence of true goodnefs.   Efteem him as a brother
and a kinfman : the fame fpirit which lives in you,
lives in him : the divine image is ftamped on him,
as well as upon you ; and he copies that amiable pattern and example, which leads all its followers to immortality and everlafting blifs.

AN

INTERESTING EPISTLE

FROM

A MARRIED GENTLEMAN

TO

HIS WIFE.

MORE than *twenty* years have elapfed, my deareft
Edwina, fince I had the favour of your hand at the
altar ; yet I feel my affection as, ftrong as ever, and
my efteem ftill higher, having been a witnefs to your
                                                    rifing

rifing above many trying circumftances, in which lefs religion and virtue than you are poffeffed of muft have failed.

It has been our good fortune, fince the time of our union, not to be obliged to be feparated from each other, fo long as to have made it neceffary for us to reprefs our fenfibility with the tedioufnefs of expecta-tion, to regret in vain the want of each other's fup-port, or the long denial of endearing converfe : Hap-py in a domeftic life, we have been divided only by thofe avocations which the care of our family and the duties of my office have rendered unavoidable, and from which we have returned in general more fatisfied with ourfelves, and with frefh pleafure to each other.

But, my deareft Edwina ! this fcene is not to laft ; we muft prepare for an alteration ; it is a theme on which we have often converfed ; death we are ap-prifed will come, and cut fhort our profpects, and perhaps overtake us before we have completed half thofe fchemes we had formed for the comfort of our-felves and our deareft connexions. What then can fupport us under the idea of this feparation ? What can reconcile us to being torn from thefe pleafing oc-cupations ? Nothing but the delightful hope of meet-ing again in a future and eternal world, where thofe feeds of happinefs, which we are now fowing, will be brought to a maturity they can never arrive at here below.

O ! what joy to be admitted to thofe feats of blifs, where there is no more pain, no more forrow, no more feparation ! Our complacency in each other will then arife from the recollection of thofe in-nocent pleafures we enjoyed together here ; but what will unite us more than any thing elfe, and will complete our felicity, will be the remembrance of all thofe

thofe mutual endeavours we exerted, to ftrengthen our good principles, and to make each other excel in virtue and religion.

This is a ftate we are warranted to afpire after, by the concurring teftimony of good and wife men in all ages of the world ; who have invariably fupported themfelves with this confolation, under the lofs of friends, that " we fhould go to them, though they cannot return to us." This is confirmed alfo by the declarations of the word of truth*. Here then let us fix our dependance ; this only can promife, with any certainty, a continuance of our happpinefs ; fo fhall we avoid thofe romantic and delufive ideas of felicity fo natural to weak minds, which never can be realized on earth : fo fhall we fecure to ourfelves the firmeft and moft lafting fupport againft that inevitable change and fhort abfence we know ourfelves deftined to fubmit to : fo fhall we obtain thofe fupreme enjoyments, which are not only eternal, but continually improving.——

THE.

* That good men fhall be united in a future ftate, a ftate of perfect purity and eternal peace, is an idea fo full of comfort and confolation, and affords us a profpect fo highly gratifying and delightful, that it is impoffible to confider it without an heartfelt exultation, which is the more unbounded, as neither reafon nor revelation forbid us to indulge it.

This hope like all thofe which we derive from the promifes of the Gofpel is given to fupport us in the trials and temptations to which we are expofed while here below, and will attend us in every fituation ; in profperity it will guard, in adverfity it will cheer us ; and as age advances, and life lofes its value, it will more and more encourage us till we arrive at the perfect day.

THE PORTRAIT

OF

A REAL FRIEND;

DRAWN FROM LIFE.

Friends grow not thick on every bough.

NIGHT THOUGHTS.

CONCERNING the man you call your friend—tell me, will he weep with you in the hour of diftrefs ? Will he faithfully reprove you to your face, for actions for which others are ridiculing or cenfuring you behind your back ? Will he dare to ftand forth in your defence, when diftraction is fecretly aiming its deadly weapons at your reputation ? Will he acknowledge you with the fame cordiality, and behave to you with the fame friendly attention, in the company of your, fuperiors in rank and fortune, as when the claims of pride or vanity do not interfere with thofe of friendfhip ?

If misfortune and loffes fhould oblige you to retire into a walk of life, in which you cannot appear with the fame diftinction, or entertain your friends with the fame liberality as formerly, will he ftill think himfelf happy in.

P 2   your.

your foeiety, and, inftead of gradually withdraw-
ing himfelf from an unprofitable connexion, take
pleafure in profeffing himfelf your friend, and cheerfully affift you to fupport the burden of your afflictions ? When ficknefs fhall call you to retire from
the gay and bufy fcenes of the world, will he follow
you into your gloomy retreat, liften with attention
to your "tale of fymptoms," and minifter the balm
of confolation to your fainting fpirit ? And laftly,
when death fhall burft afunder every earthly tie, will
he fhed a tear upon your grave, and lodge the dear
remembrance of your mutual friendfhip in his heart,
as a treafure never to be refigned ? The man who
will not do all this, may be your companion—your
flatterer—your feducer—but, depend on it, he is not
your *friend** .

THE

CONSOLATIONS OF RELIGION:

NEITHER FEW NOR SMALL.

This can fupport us all is fea befides.

NIGHT THOUGHTS.

WHILE we are in this probationary ftate of being, we *muft* encounter difficulties, and ftruggle
with

---

* A *real* friend is hardly to be met with either in profperity or adverfity, and therefore juftly compared to an
apparition, which many people talk of, but few ever faw.

with uneafinefs. The heart will often be diffatisfied we know not why, and reafon will ftand an idle fpec-tator, as if unconfcious of its power. In fuch cafes it ought to be awakened from its lethargy, and reminded of the tafk to which it is appointed. It fhould be informed of the high office it bears in the œconomy of the foul, and be made ac-quainted with the infidious vigilance of its enemies. But while we languifh under the un-eafinefs of difcontent, we cannot take a more effectu-al method to recover our peace, than to confider the infignificancy of every paffion that centres, and purfuit that terminates here below. Suppofe our earthly aims were directed to their object by the favouring gales of fortune—fuppofe our purfuits fhould be crowned with all the fuccefs that flattering hope affigns them ; yet—vain, changeable, and im-potent as we are, the fuccefs would not be worth even a moment's triumph.

While the heart turns upon an earthly axis like the perifhable ball it loves, it will be va-rioufly affected by outward influences. Some-times it will bear the fruits of gladnefs, and fometimes be the barren defert of melancholy ; one while it will be exhilirated by the funfhine of pleafure, and again it will languifh in the gloom of difcontent. The caufe of this is not only that the human heart is in itfelf changeable and uncertain, deriving its fenfations from conftitutional influences, but that the objects, if they are *earthly* objects, on which it depends for happinefs, are liable to va-riation and decay. Hence arifes the fuperiority of *religious* views. When our hopes of happinefs are fixed on one certain event : an event which, though re-mote, cannot be altered by mortal contingencies ; the heart has an invariable foundation whereon it may

securely

securely rest.   Without this resting place, we should
be tossed to and fro by every wind of fortune, the sport
of chance, and the dupes of expectation.   To this im-
moveable anchor of the soul religion directs us in the
hopes of immortality.

We know from the unerring word of divine revelation that we shall exist in another state of being, after the dissolution of this; and we are confirmed by every benevolent purpose of Providence
in the belief, that our future existence shall be
infinitely happy.   In this glorious hope the in-
terests of a temporary life are swallowed up and
lost.   This hope, like the serpent of Aaron, de-
vours the mock phantoms which are created by
the magic of this world, and at once shows the
vanity of every earthly pursuit.   Compared with
this prospect, how poor, how barren would every
scene of mortal happiness appear!   How despicable
at the best—yet how liable to be destroyed by
every storm of adversity!   For, are we not
exposed to a thousand accidents, the most trifling of which may be sufficient to break a scheme
of felicity!   Let us consider those conditions that are
almost universally desired, the dignity of the great,
and the affluence of the rich.   Are these above
the reach of misfortune?   Are they exempt from
the importunities of care!   Greatness is but the
object of impertinence and envy; and riches create
more wants than they are able to gratify.   Should
then our wishes lead to these, we should unavoidably be disappointed.   The acquisition might for a
while soothe our vanity, but we should soon sigh
for the ease of obscurity, and envy the content of those
whom pride would call our vassals.

If wealth or grandeur then cannot afford us
happiness, where shall we seek it?   Is it to be
                                found

found in the cell of the hermit ? or does it watch by the taper of folitary learning ? Loves it the fociety of laughing mirth ? or does it affect the penfive pleafures of meditation ? Is it only genuine in the cordiality of friendfhip, or in the lafting tendernefs of conjugal love ? Alas ! this train of alternatives will not do. Should we fly from the troubles of fociety to fome lonely hermitage, we fhould foon figh for the amufements of the world we had quarrelled with. The ftrongeft mind could not long fupport the burden of uncommuni-cated thought, and the firmeft heart would languifh in the ftagnation of melancholy. Afk the folitary fcholar, if ever, in his learned refearches, he be-held the retreat of happinefs—Amufement is all that he will pretend to—Amufement ! in queft of which the active powers of the mind are fre-quently worn out, the underftanding enervated by the affiduity of attention, and the memory, overburdened with uneffential ideas. Yet, poffibly, happinefs may mingle with fociety and fwell the acclamations of feftive mirth. No—the joy that dwells there cannot be called happinefs ; for the noife of mirth will vanifh with the echo of the evening, and *even in laughter the heart is fad.* If we are able to diftinguifh the ele-gance of converfation, we fhall often be difgufted with the arrogance of pride, or the impertinence of folly ; and if not, we may be amufed indeed with the noife, but can never tafte the true pleafures of fo-ciety.

As little reafon have we to hope for lafting hap-pinefs from the engagements of friendfhip, or the fweets of love. The condition of human life is at beft fo uncertain, that it is even daugerous to form any connexions that are dear. The ten-

derness

dernefs of love opens the heart to many fufferings, to many painful apprehenfions for the health and fafety of its object, and to many uneafy fenfations both from real and imaginary caufes. For want of a better remedy to thefe evils, the wifdom of ancient philofophers teacheth us to bid a brave defiance to the affaults both of pleafure and pain ; without inftructing us how to defend the heart from the inroads of forrow, or to guard againft the unfeen ftratagems of diftrefs. But the religion of a *Chriftian* affords a nobler and fafer refuge. With the exalted hopes that this prefents to us,. *the fufferings of the prefent time are not worthy to be compared.* In.thofe glorious hopes let us bury every anxious thought, the uneafinefs of difcontent, and the folicitude of care. Let us not fink under our light afflictions, which are but for a moment. A very few years, perhaps a few months or days, may bring us into that ftate of being, where care and. mifery fhall perplex no more. for ever.

Though now we may have our bed in darknefs, and our pillow on the thorn, yet the time draweth nigh when we fhall tafte of life without anguifh, and enjoy the light without *bitternefs of foul.* We are hourly hastening to that fcene of exiftence, *where the wicked ceafe from troubling, and where the weary are at reft ;* where hope fhall no more be cut off by difappointment, and where the diftreffes of time are forgotten in the endlefs joys of eternity.

LANGHORNE.

:)

MERCY

MERCY AND JUSTICE,

HAPPILY UNITED.

A God all mercy is a God unjuſt.

NIGHT THOUGHTS.

JESUS CHRIST, when he was hanging on the
croſs, thus prayed for the Jews who crucified him;
*Father, forgive them ; for they know not what they
do.* As if he had ſaid, they know not that I am
thy Son, come down from heaven to bring the
truth to them ; to redeem them from Satan's
ſlavery, and from eternal deſtruction. They believe me to be a moſt notorious liar ; an infringer on their liberties ; and a blaſphemer of thy
holy name. For this they have perſecuted me ;
and for this do they crucify me ; and therefore,
Father, I pray thee to forgive their ignorance and
blindneſs ; I pray thee to forgive them becauſe they
know not what they do.

Here Chriſt was merciful, without being unjuſt ;
for certainly, though their very blindneſs was a crime
and a dreadful one too ; yet it was not ſo heinous, as
it would have been, had they really known what they
were doing ; and therefore it was not beyond the
reach of mercy. But had he ſaid, Father, theſe people know me to be thy Son ; they know that I
came down from heaven to bring the truth to them;

to

to redeem them from Satan's flavery, and eternal dam-
nation—they know I am no liar ; no infringer on their
liberties ; no blafphemer of thy holy name,   but the
true Son of the everlafting Father : and notwithftanding this,   have they perfecuted me,   and do
they crucify me ;   yet do I pray thee, Father, to forgive them.   Had he faid this, his mercy would have
been as great a crime, as any they committed ; he
would have finned againft his Father, in wifhing him
to do an unjuft thing.   He would have been himfelf an encourager of vice, and defiring his Father to
be the fame.   His mercy would have been injuftice.
But he faid not fo ; but, *Father, forgive them, for they
know not what they do.*
  Chrift forgave Judas who betrayed him, for
the very fame reafon ; for certainly, Judas no
more believed, till after Chrift was crucified,
that he was truly the Son of God, than he
believed him to be the King of the Jews :
he took him for a conjurer (for in thofe days
there were many fuch), and told the officers when
they came to feize him, that if they did not take
great care, he would efcape from them by the help
of his magic arts.
  Amongft many errors, there is one very prevalent
with men, and even the *beft* of men too.   They affert
that it is the *will* only that makes a thing criminal ;
therefore, though a man commits a crime, if he be-
lieves that what he does is not criminal ; it fhall not
be fo in the fight of God ; neither fhall he be punifhed for it.
  This is falfe : and a very dangerous error ; for his
not knowing it to be a crime, is almoft as great a one,
as he can well commit.   Becaufe there is no knowledge neceffary to falvation, that is not within man's
reach ; therefore his not feeking that knowledge is a
crime.   If

If the *will* only made the thing criminal, few would be guilty ; for few are so impartial to themselves, as to believe they are in the wrong.

If your enemy repents him of his fault ; acknowledges it ; endeavours to make restitution ; and by the sincerity of his penitence, gives you room to think he will offend no more in the same manner ; you must forgive him, nay, serve him too, if in your power ; or you will be unmerciful ; and that mercy you deny, shall be denied to you again.

If he is hardened ; will not see his error ; makes no acknowledgement ; no restitution ; and proves by this, that he will still persist in doing you an injury ; you are then to execute strict justice on him, so far as to preserve, or justify yourself ; and to deprive him of the power to do further injury to either you, or your neighbour, otherwise, you will be answerable for the crimes which he commits.

Yet even here, you are to keep a steady eye, on *justice* only ; you must look on nothing else ; you must not bear him malice ; you must not think of revenge, or pursue any underhand methods to obtain it ; you must not belie him, scandalize him, or insult over his misfortunes ; you must not do him any private injury ; wrong him in any manner ; or act any kind of outrage against him. Your conduct must be fair, and open ; the dictates of pure justice, and self-preservation, and nothing else ; otherwise, you are more criminal than he ; because you are yourself committing the very same crimes for which you punish him.

Q.   I had

I had much rather fee my enemy repent, and mend his faults, than fee him punifhed for them ; becaufe this puts it in my power to be merciful : befides, by forgiving, and even ferving, thofe who do us an injury, we often make to ourfelves the moft fincere and unfhaken friendfhips. For he who has a foul capable of feeling himfelf in the wrong, and acknowledging his error, muft have fome fenfe of virtue and will be more deeply ftruck by an obligation from the perfon he has injured, than he could be, even by the hand of the executioner.

I was once moft grofsly affronted by a young gentleman, whom fome time after I had it greatly in my power to ferve ; he came into a houfe where I was, and directing his difcourfe to the reft of the company, told them in *my* prefence, wherein it lay fo much in my power to affift him : but added he, I cannot have the impudence to afk him, or expect that he will do it, after the fcandalous manner in which I have behaved to him.

I made not the leaft reply, but a few days afterwards did the bufinefs ; and fent for him to pay him a confiderable fum of money I had received. When he faw the money, and found what I had done, he burft into a flood of tears. None of my pretended friends, cried he, would ftir to ferve me ; and the greateft enemy I had in the world, has faved me from deftruction. . . . . . .

He went away, without being able even to thank me, or utter a word more ; and from that hour to the hour of his death, I never had a more fincere friend upon all occafions.

RURAL FELICITY.

A MORAL PICTURE DRAWN FROM HUMBLE LIFE.

ALL hail to thee ! thou peaceful lone retreat !
Welcome this rude uncultivated spot !
Where hospitality has fix'd her seat,
In humble Poverty's sequester'd cot.

Those barren hills that bound yon dreary rocks,
That solitary stream meand'ring flow,
This little pasture, and the scanty flocks,
Have charms which opulence may never know.

By servile tribes and fortune's minions scorn'd,
Remote from crowds, on schemes of grandeur bent,
Here simple Nature, sweetly unadorn'd,
Dwells with her handmaids, Virtue and Content.

Within this lowly hut, whose tottering roof
Seems just departing from its time-worn thatch,
A gen'rous pair, compassion's noblest proof,
For ev'ry trav'ller lift the friendly latch.

Tho' small their income, ample is their mind,
With few possessions they've abundant wealth ;
In Nature's bounteous lap they daily find
Life's choicest blessings, Innocence and Health.

Together

Together once they trod its early ftage,
Together now they journey down the vale ;
Paft fcenes of youth endear approaching age,
And waft them onward with a gentle gale.

One beauteous maid, dear pledge of nuptial love,
With artlefs prattle ev'ry care beguiles ;
She, while her parents cherifh and improve,
Cheers all their thoughtful hours with infant fmiles.

For her alone they wear a fhort-liv'd gloom,
Her future weal ftill anxious to fecure ;
Content, when fummon'd to their final doom,
To leave her *honeft*, tho' they leave her poor.

" O facred wedlock ! flame for ever bright !
" Perpetual fource of untumultuous joy !
" Pure, filent ftream ! that flows with new delight,
" Blifs ftill increafing, fweets that never cloy ;

" 'Midft buftling throngs, thy foft endearments charm,
" Reftrain the hufband, and protect the wife ;
" But chief thy chafte connubial raptures warm
" The peaceful current of unruffled life."

There the mild tranfports of the focial hour,
Forbid each ill completed wifh to roam,
Beft pleas'd to feek retirement's halcyon bow'r,
And rear their ripening progeny at home.

Approach this rural fcene, ye little Great,
Ye ever roving, ever thoughtlefs crew,
Sufpend awhile magnificence and ftate,
To learn contentment from the happy few.

Comey.

Come, wearied Indigence, forget thy woes,
This faithful cottage harbours no difguife ;
Here, undifturb'd, enjoy a calm repofe,
And tafte that comfort which the world denies.

---***---

DESULTORY REMARKS

ON THE

FAILINGS OF HUMAN NATURE.

WITH EXAMPLES TAKEN FROM LIFE.

Gratior et pulchro veniens in corpore virtus.   VIRGIL.

IT has long been my chief amufement to anal-
yze mankind, to ftrip them of every adventitious
advantage ; to confider them, 1st, merely as men ;
2dly, as members of fociety ; and 3dly, to clothe
them with their accidental, natural, and acquired
qualifications.   But it is a labour which by no-
Q 2   means

means perfects the *benevolent* difpofitions of the foul. For when thus examined, many characters, which are esteemed virtuous, lofe their false glofs, and appear shocking, vicious and deteftable ; while others gain infinitely by the scrutiny, and from contemptible, become admirable, and worthy of efteem and imitation. For, fuch is the ridiculoufnefs of mankind, a real good character is often defpifed for want of a few qualities, which, to the calm and unprejudiced eye of reafon, would tarnifh the luftre of all its virtues, and render it bafe and contemptible indeed.

Give me leave to inftance in two men, with whom I have long maintained fome degree of intimacy. Pancris is generous, affable, and courageous. He knows not fear. The general tenor of his life has been fuch as renders him, at leaft in the opinion of the generality of his fellow-creatures, equally a ftranger to timidity and fhame. He poffeffes many valuable accomplifhments of learning, wit, ftrength, genius, and a found judgment.— Wherever he comes, his fallies of humour, infallibly ' fet the table in a roar.' His learning makes his company agreeable to philofophers ; and his gaiety, to all who prefer the wild effufions of fancy and vivacity, before the argumentative fedatenefs of fober reafon.

I need not fay, that he is every-where received with fuch a warmth of friendfhip, as declares his prefence in a great meafure effential to the happinefs of his acquaintances. The recital of ' a tender tail of woe will fo roufe his compaffion and generofity, as to prove that he ' feels and bleeds at every pore.' To the utmoft of his power he relieves every misfortune, and alleviates every diftrefs ; and feldom do the unfortunate leave his gate without

without eyes fwimming with the tears of gratitude, without invoking the choiceft. bleffings of heaven upon his head.

Thus far he feems to be the moft highly fin-. ifhed tranfcript of human perfection; but, how reluctantly muft. we examine the other fide of his character !

His figure is elegant;, almoft beyond imagination. He is the idol of the fair fex ; and often has he ufed their prepoffeffion in his favour to effectuate their ruin. Many. have hung upon his tongue,, which, like Belial's,

Dropt manna, and could make the worfe appear.
The better reafon---
————His thoughts were
To vice induftrious.   MILTON'S Par. Loft.

They heard, and declared their folly with the lofs of virtue, fame and honour ; while he, to atone for his crimes, has killed in duels feveral defenders of the injured. By the fword has he cut off the hopes of blooming youth, and brought down the grey hairs of many an aged. parent with forrow to the grave.

Tranquillius, his neighbour, is a very different character—His acquaintances are few and thofe who diftinguifh his worth are ftill fewer. He poffeffes every valuable endowment, which is fitted to fmoothe his paffage through ' the cool fequeftered vale of life.' His fortune is not large, but fufficient; with œconomy, to enable him to appear with *eclat* in the country, where he always refides. But, to experience that godlike pleafure, to give, he abridges himfelf of what many account the *neceffaries* of life.

He

He proves himself to be an univerfal and practical
philanthropift, by a judicious diftribution of his riches.   He feldom appears without enjoying the ineffa-
ble happinefs of hearing multitudes of the fons of
Poverty and Woe acknowledge him their friend,
their benefactor ; and clamorous in prayers to heaven in his behalf ; and others, whofe feelings are too
big for utterance, declare by their looks what words
could never exprefs.   There is an affability in his
behaviour, which is the genuine offspring, nay the
diftinguifhing characteriftic of the moft confummate
benevolence.   He is rather an Heraclitus, than a
Democritus, feeming to have modelled his imitative
powers like Jaques ; for I have feen him.

————As he lay along
Under an oak whofe antique root peeps out,
Upon the brook that brawls along the wood,
        *   *   *   *

Augmenting it with tears.   SHAKESPEAR.

His converfation is never agreeable to the juvenile
and fprightly ; for, in defpite of themfelves, it would
make them ferious and thoughtful.   By the young,
the gay, and thofe who have fpent their time in the
purfuit of trifles, fo as to be overtaken by old age, before they have left the follies of youth, he is
defpifed.   He is accuftomed to dwell frequently on the contemplation of human miferies, and

To feel for all the woes of all mankind.

He cannot therefore commit what would give any of
the fpecies a *momentary* uneafinefs, much lefs plant
ftings and daggers in their hearts.   His learning is
                                                  very

very profound and extenfive, his genius penetrating, and his judgment ftrong.

Educated in a college, far from the fcenes of active life, he contracted the habit of thinking; in confequence of which, when apparent dangers threaten, he feels them almoft as feverely as if they had already befallen him. He is exceffively timid, and very careful and folicitous to avoid every appearance of evil. He is not in the leaft indebted to nature for an exterior, which is the moft grotefque imaginable; he is low in ftature, very corpulent, and frequently the butt of ridicule on thefe accounts. Yet ftill he is truly a worthy character, and deferving general efteem.

ELEGY TO PITY.

HAIL, lovely power! whofe bofom heaves a figh,
When fancy paints the fcene of deep diftrefs,
Whofe tears fpontaneous cryftallize the eye,
When rigid fate denies the power to blefs.

Not all the fweets Arabia's gales convey
From flowery meads, can with that figh compare;
Not dew-drops glittering in the morning ray,
Seem near fo beauteous as that falling tear.

Devoid of fear the fawns around thee play;
Emblem of peace, the dove before thee flies:
No blood-ftain'd traces mark thy blamelefs way,
Beneath thy feat no haplefs infect dies.

Come,

Come, lovely nymph ! and range the fields with me,
To fpring the partridge from the guileful foe,
From fecret fnares the ftruggling bird to free,
And ftop the hand uprais'd to give the blow.

And when the air with heat meridian glows,
And nature droops beneath the fcorching gleam,
Let us, flow wandering where the current flows,
Save finking flies that float along the ftream.

Or turn to nobler, greater tafks thy care,
To me thy fympathetic gifts impart ;
Teach me in friendfhip's woes to claim a fhare ;
And juftly boaft the generous feeling heart*.

Teach me to footh the helplefs orphan's grief,
With timely aid the widow's tears affuage,
To mifery's moving cries to yield relief,
And be the fure fupport of drooping age.

So when the cheerful fpring of life fhall fade,
And finking nature owns the dread decay,
Some foul congenial then may lend its aid,
And gild the clofe of life's eventful day.

---

* Sympathy and compaffion are the offspring of Heaven ;
to weep with them that weep is the duty of all.

REMARKABLE.

REMARKABLE INSCRIPTION

ON A

TOMB-STONE, AT GREEN-BAY, JAMAICA.

HERE lieth the body of Lewis Gauldy, Efq. who departed this life at Port Royal, Dec. 22, 1739, aged 80. He was born at Montpelier, in France, but left that country for his religion, and came to fettle in this ifland, when he was fwallowed up in the great earthquake in 1692, and by the providence of God was by another fhock thrown into the fea, and miraculoufly faved by fwimming, until a boat took him up. He lived many years after in great repu- tation, beloved by all that knew him, and much la- mented at his death.

> God moves in a myfterious way,
> His wonders to perform ;
> He plants his footfteps in the fea,
> And rides upon the ftorm.

EMPLOYMENTS

EMPLOYMENTS SUITED TO

GENTLEMEN,

WHETHER IN *TOWN* OR *COUNTRY;*

TO PREVENT TIME BEING A BURDEN TO THEM.

'Tis a difficult thing to be idle and innocent.

PERSONS who by birth, marriage, death of relatives, or fuccefs in bufinefs, are become the poffeffors of independent fortunes, and confequently entitled *gentlemen;* may experience it dufficult, at times, to find employments for the many leifure hours they apparently have upon their hands from day to day. But this I apprehend would feldom be the cafe, if the duties we owe to our Creator, ourfelves, and our fellow-creatures, were properly attended to and regarded.

The dictates of piety, virtue, benevolence, and humanity, will ever fuggeft ample matter for the exercife of our mental powers and faculties ; while at the fame time they may fuitably point out to us objects well deferving our notice and purfuit.

Reflections on the works of creation daily prefented to our view ; reading judicious and approved authors on moral and entertaining fubjects, fuch as *hiftory, geography, aftronomy, philofophy,* and the polite arts ; writing letters to felect friends ; or, if there is a tafte for it, *drawing, defigning pictures, painting,*
and

and *music; walking or riding* out when the weather permits ; *converfation* with perfons of learning, ingenuity, and experience ; finding out and relieving the neceffitous and diftreft*; thefe are innocent, rational, and commendable employments, exercifes, and recreations, fit for gentlemen† whether in town or country, and in all feafons of the year ; which may keep both the mind and body ufefully engaged at all times, and promote health, cheerfulnefs, and the benefit of fociety in general.

As habits of indolence and inactivity cannot be too carefully avoided, by the poffeffors of wealth and abundance ; fo ufeful, praifeworthy, and ornamental accomplifhments and purfuits cannot be too zealoufly encouraged and promoted ; as truly beneficial to individuals in particular, and the community at large. G. W.

ON

* 'Tis more bleffed to *give* then to *receive* ; the inward fatisfaction and complacency naturally attending the relieving a worthy object of compaffion, is truly its own reward.

†The real gentleman will be as choice of his amufements and recreations, as of his company and connexions ; he will be as careful not to difgrace his character by the diverfions he countenances and partakes of, as of the perfons he chufes as his intimate friends ; well affured, either of them may (if improper) ruin his character, reputation, and eftate.

R

ON CONTEMPT, OR DESPISING OUR

INFERIORS.

Defpife no one, but look at home.

THAT which conftitutes an object of contempt to the ill-natured and malevolent, becomes the object of other paffions to a worthy and good-natured man ; for in fuch a perfon, wickednefs and vice muft always raife hatred and abhorrence ; while weaknefs and folly will ever be fure to excite pity and compaffion.

However deteftable this quality, which is a mixture of pride and ill-nature, may appear when confidered in the ferious fchool of Heraclitus, it will prefent no lefs abfurd and ridiculous an idea to the laughing fect of Democritus, efpecially as we may obferve, that the meaneft and bafeft of all human beings are generally the moft forward to defpife others. So that the moft contemptible are generally the moft contemptuous.

As a good man, as I have before obferved, will give no entertainment to any fuch a paffion ; fo neither will a fenfible man, I am well perfuaded, find much opportunity to exert it. If men would make but a moderate ufe of that felf-examination, which philofophers and divines have recommended to them, it would tend greatly to the cure of this difpofition. Their contempt would then perhaps as their charity is faid to do, begin at *home*. To fay the truth, a man hath this better chance of defpifing himfelf, than he hath of defpifing others, as he is likely to know himfelf beft. . . . .

Contempt

Contempt is generally mutual : there is scarce any one man who despises another, without being at the same time despised by him, of which I shall endeavour to produce some few instances.

As the right honourable lord Squanderfield, at the head of a vast retinue, passes by Mr. M. Buckram, citizen and taylor, in his chaise and *one*, " See there!" says my lord, with an air of the highest contempt, " that rascal Buckram, with his fat wife : I suppose he is going to his country house, for such fellows must have their country house, as well as their vehicle. These are the rascals that complain of want of trade." Buckram, on the other hand, is no sooner recovered from the fear of being run over, before he could get out of the way ; than, turning to his wife, he cries, " Very fine, faith ! an honest citizen is to be run over by such fellows as these, who drive about their coaches and six with other people's money. See, my dear, what an equipage he has got, and yet he cannot find money to pay an honest tradesman. He is above an *hundred* pounds deep in my books ; how I despise such lords !"

Lady Fanny Rantum, from the side-box, casting her eyes on an honest pawnbroker's wife below her, bids lady Betty her companion take notice of that creature in the pit ; " Did you ever see, lady Betty," says she, " such a strange wretch ? how the awkward monster is dressed ?" The good woman at the same time surveying lady Fanny, and offended, perhaps, at a scornful smile, which she sees in her countenance, whispers her friend, " Observe lady Fanny Rantum. As great airs as that fine lady gives herself, my husband hath all her jewels under lock and key ; what a contemptible thing is *poor* quality !"

Is there on earth a greater object of contempt than the poor scholar to a splendid beau ? unless perhaps the

the fplendid beau to the poor fcholar ! The philofopher and the world; the man of bufinefs and the man
of pleafure; the beauty and the wit; the hypocrite
and the profligate; the covetous and the fquanderer;
are all alike inftances of this reciprocal contempt.

Take the fame obfervations into the loweft life, and
we fhall find the fame pronenefs to defpife each other.
The common foldier, who hires himfelf out to be
fhot at for *five-pence* a day, who is the only flave in a
free country; and is liable to be fent to any part of
the world without his confent; and whilft at home
fubject to the fevereft punifhments, for offences which
are not to be found in our law books; yet this noble
perfonage looks with a contemptuous air on all his
brethren of that order in the commonwealth, whether of mechanics or hufbandmen, from whence he was
himfelf taken.   On the other hand, however adorned with his brick-duft coloured coat, and bedaubed
with worfted lace of a penny a yard, the very *gentle-*
man foldier is as much defpifed in his turn, by the
whiftling carter, who comforts himfelf, that he is a
free-born Englifhman, and will live with no mafter
any longer than he likes him; nay, and though he
never was worth ten pounds in his life, is ready
to anfwer a captain, if he offends him, " D—n you,
Sir, who are you ? is it not we that pay you ?"

This contemptuous difpofition is in reality the
fure attendant on a mean and bad mind in every ftation; on the contrary, a great and *good* man will be
free from it, whether he be placed at the top or bottom of life.   I was therefore not a little pleafed with
a rebuke lately given by a blackfhoe boy to another,
who had expreffed his contempt of one of the modern
town-fmarts : " Why fhould you defpife him, Jack ?"
faid the honeft lad : " we are all what the Lord
pleafed to make us."   TOM

TOM TURF;

A NEWMARKET CHARACTER,

TAKEN FROM LIFE.

A man with more money than wit.

TOM TURF is possessed of an estate of *fifteen hundred* pounds a year, which is just sufficient to furnish him with a variety of riding frocks, jockey boots, smart hats, and coach whips. Tom's great ambition is to be deemed a *jemmy fellow*; he therefore appears always in a morning in a *Newmarket* frock, a short bob wig, neat buckskin breeches, and white silk stockings.

He keeps a *phaeton* and four handsome *bays*, a stable of hunters; and a pack of hounds in the country. The reputation of being a good coachman, and driving a set of horses with skill; or, in his own phrase, *doing his business well*, he esteems the greatest character in life; and thinks himself seated on the very pinnacle of glory, when he is mounted in a high chaise at a horse-race. *Newmarket* has not a more active spirit; he is there, frequently his *own* jockey, and always boasts, as a singular accomplishment, *that he does not ride above eight stone and a half.*

He is a little man not of a very healthy constitution, but wishes to be thought capable of the greatest fatigue, and is perpetually laying wagers of the vast journies he can perform in a day. He

R 2

has

has likewife an ambition to be reckoned a man of confummate-debauch, and endeavours to make you believe, that he never goes to bed without firft drinking *three* or *four* bottles of claret, lying with as many wh——es, and knocking down as many watch-men*. He very often comes drunk into one of the theatres, about the middle of the third act, and heroically expofes himfelf to the hiffes of both the galleries.

When he meets you, he generally begins with defcribing his laft night's debauch, or relates the arrival of a new wh–re upon the town, or entertains you with the exploits of his *bay cattle ;* and if you decline converfing with him on thefe *improving* fubjects, he fwears you are a fellow of no foul or genius, and ever afterwards fhuns your company. From fuch defpicable characters, good Lord deliver us.

ON A LIFE OF PLEASURE.

FROM A YOUNG LADY IN DORSETSHIRE TO HER FRIEND

IN LONDON.

I WRITE, my dear friend, from this agreeable folitude ; the meadows and gardens, the thick gloom of the trees, the dafhing of the cafcade ; all thefe objects, fo unufual to me, give an agreeable fort of melancholy to the mind.

Among

---

* Thefe exploits are leading features in the character of a modern young man of fpirit,

Among very different fcenes and different company, my fair correfpondent, I doubt not, paffes
her days.

At one period fhe receives company, at another
fhe is dreffing for the opera. One hour fhe liftens
to the jefts of fome *petitmaitre*, and the next to the
vivacity of her female vifitants. When fhe lies
down to reft, her thoughts are engroffed—all engroffed by *plays*, *routs*, *auctions*, and *chard-tables*.
It is no wonder if the devotions of the evening
are wholly neglected, or at leaft performed in a
flight and carelefs manner.

Could my dear Sophia have imagined *twelve*
months fince, that I fhould have fent her fuch a
letter ? But I have not now taken up the pen in
a vein of raillery. I am of late grown more than
ordinarily penfive. Much of my paft time has been
fpent, I muft acknowledge with regret, in diffipation. and *falfe* pleafure. I am now refolved, with
the affiftance of divine wifdom, to act like a being
endowed with rational faculties, and formed to live
for ever. I perufe, with the greateft diligence,
night and morning, the facred writings ; and am
quite enamoured with the excellence of the precepts contained in them ; and with the exalted
idea they give of our Creator, Preferver, and Re-
deemer.

Ye gay companions of my former life ! your
dream of happinefs will very fpeedily vanifh away
like the dew of the morning. Why will ye per-
fift in your thoughtlefs courfe ? " Be affured the
years will foon draw nigh, when ye fhall have no
pleafure in them : and the days when the keepers
of the houfe fhall tremble, and the ftrong men bow
themfelves ; when the mourners fhall go about the
ftreets ; when the duft fhall return to its native duft,

and

and the spirit to God who gave it." The tolling knell often proclaims the demise of an intimate friend or neighbour; but you hear it void of sensibility and reflection.

The retrospect of a life spent in gaiety and amusement will afford no complacence, no serenity in the views of death* ; but the retrospect of a life of rational devotion will be truly delightful even at that awful crisis. "The hour is come (the believer may then say), the happy hour I have so ardently expected. I have learned to acquiesce in every disposal of infinite wisdom.

What is persecution or exile, or even death itself, to the real Christian? What are the best delights of human life? Mere anxiety and vexation; but the delights of futurity have no diminution, and are such as I cannot, in the present mode of existence, form any competent idea of.

May my dear Sophy be persuaded to steal from the giddy multitude, and enjoy that best of converse, which fallible and weak-sighted human beings are too apt to neglect or despise—converse with her own *heart*. Hence she will learn humility, resignation, penitence, and gratitude†. May all her devout exercises be more acceptable than incense from the altar, to that Power who is ever willing to hear, and to fulfil the requests of the sincerely penitent.

I am, dear friend, your real well-wisher, &c.
MATILDA F——.

Winbourn, Dorsetshire.

THE

---

*The propriety of this lady's sentiments no gentleman in his right senses can deny.

†Good was the advice of King David, *Commune with thy own heart* Psalm iv. 4.

THE

INCONVENIENCES OF A COUNTRY LIFE.

AN EXTRACT.

THE witty duke of Buckingham, meeting one
day with a fnarling dog in the ftreets, faid, " D——n
you, I wifh you was married, and fettled in the
country ;'' which the duke thought the greateft
curfe he could wifh any one. As I have lately removed there for cheapnefs, I will relate what I have
met with.

A friend I had confulted, hired for me a fmall
farm, which he faid would aflift me in houfekeeping;
and my wife was pleafed with the thoughts of having
her own pigs and poultry. I found the country as
full of brutality as dirt ; there is not more clay in
the roads than knavery in the inhabitants; and the
whole fo fortified in ruftic impudence, that I proteft
the hackney-coachman and draymen in London are
better companions. The cows I bought had flunk
their calves, the fheep were rotten, the horfes broken-
winded, the hogs mangy, and the poultry had the
droop ; yet they were all fold to me with the greateft
afleverations of perfection.

Then, as to provifions, the butcher calls once a
week, to know what meat you want, and that day
fe'nnight brings you a buttock of beef of 30lb.
weight, when ten was all you wanted ; and as the
family is fmall, he gives you meat not much better
than carrion, but does not forget to charge the higheft

eft price for it. As to fish, we get none but what ftinks, though only ten miles from the fea; and my landlord shewed me a very pretty pond, as he called it, which would at any time, he said, afford me a dish of fish. This coft me 40s. for a net, in order to get fifteen penny worth of carp, as big as my finger.

Another recommendation of his farm was its being situated in a *fine sporting country*; I had a mind to try it; and therefore bought a dog and a gun; and going out one morning, was met by the squire's gamekeeper, who desired me to walk home immediately, or he muft shoot my dog. Well, to be sure, there is no end of the happiness of the country: I lately took to *gardening*, and had scarce cropped my kitchen ground, before a neighbouring squire rode his fox-hounds through it; and upon my consulting a lawyer for a profecution, I found the matter would be tried by a jury of fox-hunters.

Every fellow in the neighbourhood marks you for his prey, and will treat you with infolence, if you do not pay in every thing through the nofe, like a lord or a nabob. One had need be made of money, for the moment there is a want of this, our cattle are pounded, the pigs worried, the fences broken down, and our hen-roofts robbed. A pretty life for a man of *small* fortune! No, no, let none but men of *wealth* think of it; I could live in town upon one hundred pounds a year, much better than in the country upon *three*; every pig I have killed has coft me a guinea; and I had better pay five shillings a-head for poultry, than bring them up at home. . . . .

So much for *gentlemen* farmers.

THE

HUMBLE AND CONTENTED MAN.

A POEM, ADDRESSED TO A FRIEND.

A FLOW of good fpirits I've feen, with a fmile,
  To worth make a fhallow pretence ;
And the chat of good-breeding with eafe for awhile
  May pafs for good-nature and fenfe ;

But where is the bofom untainted by art,
  The judgment fo modeft and ftaid,
That union fo rare of the head and the heart,
  Which fixes the friends it has made ?

Should fortune capricioufly ceafe to be coy,
  And in torrents of plenty defcend ;
I doubtlefs like others fhould clafp her with joy,
  And my wants and my wifhes extend*.

But fince 'tis deny'd me, and Heaven beft knows
  Whether kinder, to grant it or not,
Say why fhould I vainly difturb my repofe,
  And peevifhly carp at my lot ?

Many men of lefs worth—you good natur'dly cry—
  To fplendour and opulence foar :
Suppofe I allow it, yet, pray Sir, am I
  Lefs happy becaufe they are more ?

---

* It is generally obferved, our wifhes enlarge as our wealth increafes.

Nor e'er may my pride or my folly reflect
  On the fav'rites whom fortune has made,
Regardless of thousands who pine with neglect,
  In pensive obscurity's shade,

With whom, when comparing the merit I boast,
  Tho' rais'd by indulgence to fame,
I sink in confusion bewilder'd and loft,
  And I wonder I am what I am ;

And what are these wonders, these blessings refin'd,
  Which splendour and opulence shower ?
The health of the body, and peace of the mind,
  Are things which are out of their power.

To Contentment's calm sunshine, the lot of the few,
  Can insolent Greatness pretend ?
Or can it bestow what I boast of in you,
  That blessing of blessings—a *friend* ?

ON THE

PLEASURES AND ADVANTAGES

OF

READING AND CONVERSATION,

IN THE SUPERIOR WALKS OF LIFE.

At the head of all the pleasures which offer themselves to the man of liberal education, may confi-
dently be placed that derived from *books*.   In variety,
                                        durability,

durability, and facility of attainment, no other can
ftand in competition with it. Imagine that we had
it in our power to call up the fhades of the greateft
and wifeft men that ever exifted, and oblige them to
converfe with us on the moft interefting topics—
what an ineftimable privilege fhould we think it !
how fuperior to all common enjoyments ! But in
a well-furnifhed library we, in fact, poffefs this power.

We can queftion Xenophon and Cæfar on their
campaigns, make Demofthenes and Cicero plead
before us, join in the audience of Socrates and Plato,
and receive demonftrations from Euclid and Newton*. In books we have the choiceft thoughts of
the ableft men in their beft drefs. We can at pleafure exclude dulnefs and impertinence, and open
our doors to wit and good fenfe alone.

If domeftic enjoyments have contributed in the firft
degree to the happinefs of my life (and I fhould be
ungrateful not to acknowledge that they have), the
pleafures of *reading* have beyond all queftion held the
fecond place. Without books I have never been able
to pafs fcarce a fingle day to my entire fatisfaction ;
with them, no day has been fo dull as not to have
its pleafure. Even pain and ficknefs have for a time
been charmed away by them. By the eafy provifion
of a book, I have frequently worn through long nights
and days of pain, with all the difference in my feelings
between calm content and fretful impatience. Such
occurrences have afforded me full proof of the poffibility of being cheaply pleafed and inftructed at the
fame time.

S   Reading

---

*Well may it be afferted by an eminent writer, by *reading*
we converfe with the dead, by *converfation* with the living,
and by *contemplation* with ourfelves.

Reading may in every senſe be called a *cheap* amuſe‐ment. A *taſte for books*, indeed, may be made expen‐ſive enough ; but that is only where there is a taſte for *fine editions, bindings, paper,* and *type**. Learn to diſtinguiſh between books to be *peruſed*, and books to be *poſſeſſed*. Of the former, you may find an ample ſtore in every ſubſcription library, the proper uſe of which to a ſcholar is to furniſh his mind, without loading his ſhelves. No apparatus, no appointment of time and place, is neceſſary for the enjoyment of reading. From the midſt of buſtle and buſineſs you may, in an inſtant, by the magic of a book plunge into ſcenes of remote ages and coun‐tries, and diſengage yourſelf from preſent care and fa‐tigue. "Sweet pliability of man's ſpirit," (cries Sterne, on relating an occurrence of this kind in his Sentimental Journey,) " that can at once ſurrender itſelf to illuſions, which cheat expectation and ſorrow of their weariſome moments !

The next of the rational pleaſures of life that I ſhall point out, is that of *converſation*.—This is a pleaſure of higher zeſt than that of reading ; ſince in converſ‐ing we not only receive the ſentiments of others, but impart our own, and from this reciprocation a ſpirit and intereſt ariſe, which books cannot give in an equal degree. Fitneſs for converſation muſt depend on the ſtore of ideas laid up in the mind, and the faculty of communicating them. Theſe, in a great degree, are the reſults of education and the habit of ſociety : and to a certain point they are favoured by ſuperiority of condition. But this is only to a *certain* point ; for when you arrive at that claſs in which ſenſuality, in‐dolence, and diſſipation, are foſtered by exceſs of opu‐

lence,

---

* Books ſhould be choſen for the *good ſenſe* they contain, and not for their binding, be it ever ſo good.

lence*, you lofe more by diminifhed energy of mind, than you gain by fuperior refinement of manners and elegance of expreffion.

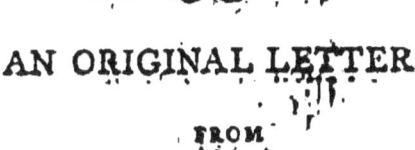

AN ORIGINAL LETTER

FROM

DR. JOHNSON TO AN INTIMATE FRIEND,

ON THE DEATH OF HIS WIFE.

DEAR SIR, *March* 17, 1752.

NOTWITHSTANDING the warnings of philo-fophers, and the daily examples of loffes and misfor-tunes which life forces upon us, fuch is the abforption of our thoughts in the bufinefs of the prefent day—fuch the refignation of our reafon to empty hopes of future felicity—or fuch our unwillingnefs to forefee what we dread, that every calamity comes fuddenly upon us, and not only preffes us as a burden but crufh-es as a blow.

There are evils which happen out of the common courfe of nature, againft which it is no reproach not to be provided. A flafh of lightning intercepts the traveller in his way. The concuffion of an earth-quake heaps the ruins of cities upon their inhabitants. But other miferies time brings, though filently, yet vifibly forward, by its own lapfe, which yet approach-es unfeen, becaufe we turn our eyes away : and feize us

---

* This is too often the cafe among the great.

us unresisted, because we could not arm ourselves a-
gainst them, but by setting them before us.

That it is in vain to shrink from what cannot be a-
voided, and to hide that from ourselves which must
sometimes be found, is a truth which we all know,
but which all neglect ; and perhaps none more than
the speculative reasoner, whose thoughts are always
from home, whose eye wanders over life, whose fancy dances after meteors of happiness kindled by itself, and who examines every thing rather than his
own state.

Nothing is more evident than that the decays of
age must terminate in death.   Yet there is no man
(says Tully) who does not believe that he may yet
live another year ; and there is none who does not upon the same principle, hope another year for his parent
or friend : but the fallacy will be in time detected ;
the *last* year, the *last* day, will come ; it has come,
and is past.   " The life which made my own life
pleasant is at an end, and the gates of death are shut
upon my prospects."

The loss of a friend, on whom the heart was fixed, to whom every wish and endeavour tended, is a
state of desolation in which the mind looks abroad
impatient of itself, and finds nothing but emptiness
and horror.   The blameless life—the artless tenderness—the pious simplicity—the modest resignation—
the patient sickness, and the quiet death—are remembered only to add value to the loss—to aggravate regret for what cannot be amended—to deepen
sorrow for what cannot be recalled..

These are the calamities by which Providence
gradually disengages us from the love of life.   Other evils fortitude may repel, or hope may mitigate ;
but irreparable privation leaves nothing to exercise re-
solution, or flatter expectation.   The dead cannot
                                        return,.

return, and nothing is left us here but languishment and grief.

Yet such is the course of nature, that whoever lives long must outlive those whom he loves and honours. Such is the condition of our present existence, that life must one time lose its associations, and every inhabitant of the earth must walk downward to the grave alone, and unregarded, without any partner of his joy or grief, without any interchange of his misfortunes or success. Misfortunes indeed he may yet feel, for where is the bottom of the misery of man! but what is success to him who has none to enjoy it? Happiness is not found in *self*-contemplation; it is perceived only when it is reflected from another.

We know little of the state of departed souls, because such knowledge is not necessary to a good life. Reason deserts us at the brink of the grave, and gives no farther intelligence. Revelation is not wholly silent: " There is joy among the angels of heaven over a sinner that repenteth." And surely the joy is not incommunicable to souls disentangled from the body, and made like angels.

Let hope, therefore, dictate, what Revelation does not confute—that the union of souls may still remain; and that we, who are struggling with sin, sorrow, and infirmities, may have one part in the attention and kindness of those who have finished their course, and are now receiving their reward.

These are the great occasions which force the mind to take refuge in religion. When we have no help in ourselves, what can remain but that we look up to a higher and a greater Power? And to what hope may we not raise our eyes and hearts, when we consider that the *greatest power is the best?*

Surely

Surely there is no man who, thus afflicted, does
not feek.fuccour in the Gofpel, which has brought
life and immortality to light ? The precepts of Epi-
curus, which teach us to endure what the laws of
the univerfe make neceffary, may. filence, but not.
content us.   The dictates of Zeno, who commands
us to look with indifference on abftract things, may
difpofe us to conceal our forrow, but cannot affuage
it.   Real alleviation of the lofs of friends, a rational tranquility in the profpect of our own dift o-
tion, can be received only from the promife of Him
in whofe hands are life and death ; and from the af-
furances of another and better ftate, in which all tears
will be wiped from our eyes, and the whole foul fhall
be filled with joy—Philofophy may infufe ftubborn-
nefs, but *Religion* only can give patience.

SAM. JOHNSON.

ON

THE PLEASURES OF BENEVOLENCE.

TO guard againft the fatal effects which difappointments are apt to have upon the mind, is a point
of the utmoft. confequence towards paffing through
life with any tolerable degree of comfort and fatisfaction ; for difappointments, more or lefs, muft be
the lot of all.

At the firft entrance into the world, when the imagination is active, the affections warm, and the heart
a ftranger to deceit, and confequently to fufpicion,
what delightful dreams of happinefs are formed !
Whatever may be the object in which that happinefs

is

is fuppofed' to confift, that object is purfued with ardour: the gay and thoughtlefs feek for it in diffipation and amufement ; the ambitious in power, fame, and honours ; the affectionate in love and friendfhip : but how few are there who find in any of thefe objects that happinefs which they expected !

Pleafure, fame, riches, &c. even when they are obtained, ftill leave a void in the foul, which continually minds the poffeffor that this is not the happinefs for which he was formed, and even the beft affections are liable to numberlefs difappointments, and often productive of the fevereft pangs.

The unfufpecting heart forms attachments before reafon is capable of judging whether the objects of them are fuch as are qualified to make it happy; and it often happens, that the fatal truth is not difcovered till the affections are engaged too far to be recalled, and then the difappointment muft prove a lafting forrow.

The young are too apt to fancy that the affections of their hearts will prove the fource of nothing but pleafure ; thofe who are father advanced in life, are much too apt to run into the contrary extreme. The error of the firft, even taking it in the worft light, is productive of fome pleafure, as well as pain ; that of the laft ferves only to throw a damp over every pleafure, and can be productive of nothing but pain. It leads indeed to the moft fatal confequences fince it tends to make *felf* the only object ; and the heart which is merely felfifh, muft ever be incapable of virtue and of happinefs, and a ftranger to all the folid joys of affection and benevolence ; without which the happieft ftate in this world muft be infipid, and with which even the fevereft afflictions may be eafily fupported.

In

In every state of life, in spite of every disappointment, these should still be cherished and encouraged; for though they may not always bestow such pleasures as the romantic imaginations of youth had painted, yet they will still bestow such as can be found in nothing else in this world.

Those who are freed from cares and anxieties, who are surrounded by all the means of enjoyment, and whose pleasures present themselves without being sought for, are often unhappy in the midst of all; merely because that activity of mind, in the proper exercise of which our happiness consists, has in them no object on which it may be employed. But when the heart is sincerely and affectionately interested for the good of others, a new scene of action is continually open, every moment may be employed in some pleasing and useful pursuit.

New opportunities of doing good are continually presenting themselves; new schemes are formed and ardently pursued; and even when they do not succeed, though the disappointment may give pain, yet the pleasure of self-approbation will remain; and the pursuit will be remembered with satisfaction. The next opportunity which offers itself will be readily embraced, and will furnish a fresh supply of pleasures; such pleasures as are secure from that weariness and disgust, which sooner or later are the consequences of all such enjoyments as tend merely to gratify the selfish passions and inclinations; and which always attend on an inactive state of mind, from whatever cause it may proceed.

Even in the most trifling scenes of common life, the truly benevolent may find many pleasures which would pass unnoticed by others; and in a conversation, which to the thoughtless and inattentive would afford only a trifling amusement, or perhaps no a-

musement

mufement, at all, *they* may find many fubjects for pleafing and ufeful reflections, which may conduce both to their happinefs and advantage.

It is a pleafing as well as ufeful exerc?e to the mind, to difcover real merit, through the ?eil which humility and modefty throw over it*; and to admire true greatnefs of foul, eve? i? ?he meaneft fitua-?ations in life ; or whe?? it ?? ??tfelf on occafions ???ofed to be trifl???? ?? ?herefore, in general, but ??? ??tended t? ?? ??garded.

———◦⟨◇⟩◦———

ON THE LOVE OF LIFE.

AN ESSAY.

———

Our wifhes lengthen as our fun declines.

NIGHT THOUGHTS.

———

AGE, that leffens the enjoyments of life, increafes our defire of living. Thofe dangers which in the vigour of youth we had learned to defpife, affume new terrors as we grow old. Our caution increaf-ing as our years increafe, fear at laft becomes the prevailing paffion of the mind, and the fmall remain-der of life is taken up in ufelefs efforts to keep off our end, or provide for a continued exiftence.

Strange contradiction in our nature, and to which even the wife are liable ! If I fhould judge of that part of life which lies before me by that which I

have

———

* There is no *real* merit without this veil.

have already feen, the profpect is hideous. Experience tells me that my paft enjoyments have brought
no real felicity, and fenfation affures me, that thofe
I have felt are ftronger than thofe which are yet
to come. Yet experience and fenfation in vain per-
fuade ; hope, more powerful than either, dreffes out
the diftant profpect in fancied beauty ; fome happinefs in long perfpective, ftill beckons me to purfue ; and like a lolong gamefter, every new difappointment increafes my ardour to continue the
game.

Whence then is this increafed love of life, which
grows upon us with our years ? whence comes it
that we thus make greater efforts to preferve our
exiftence, at a period when it becomes fcarce worth
the keeping ? Is it, that Nature, attentive to the pre-
fervation of mankind, increafes our wifhes to live,
while fhe leffens our enjoyments ? and as fhe robs
the fenfes of every pleafure, equips Imagination in
the fpoils? Life would be infupportable to an old
man, who, loaded with infirmities, feared death no
more than when in the vigour of manhood ; the
numberlefs calamities of decaying nature, and the
confcioufnefs of furviving every pleafure and enjoyment, would at once induce him with his own
hand to terminate the fcene of mifery ; but happily
the contempt of death forfakes him, at a time when
it could only be prejudicial ; and life acquires an
imaginary value, in proportion as its *real* value is no
more.

Our attachment to every object around us increafes, in general from the length of our acquaintance
with it*." I would not chufe," fays a French philofo-
                                        pher,

_____

* The longer we know our friends, and find them to be
really fcub, the more unwilling we fhall be to part with
them.

pher, "to fee an old poft pulled up with which I
had been long acquainted." A mind long habitua-
ted to a certain fet of objects, infenfibly becomes fond
of feeing them ; vifits them from habit, and parts
from them with reluctance : from hence proceeds
the avarice of the old in every kind of poffeffion ;
they love the world and all that it produces ; they
love life and all its advantages ; not merely becaufe
gives them pleafure but becaufe they have known
it long.

SONNET TO TIME.

INSATIATE Defpot ! whofe refiftlefs arm
  Shatters the loftieft fabric from its bafe ;
And tears from beauty ev'ry magic charm,
  And robs proud Nature of her lovelieft grace !

Still art thou kind ; for as thy pow'r prevails,
  And age comes onward, menacing decay ;
As warmth expires, and numbing froft affails,
  And life's faint lamp prefents a quiv'ring ray ;

'Tis thine to reconcile the tranquil breaft,
  To prove that fublunary joys are vain ;
  To turn from pomp, and all its tinfel train,
  And feek the filent paths of *mental* reft ;
So, from the deadlieft poifon, chymic art
  Extracts a healing balm to tranquilize the heart.

DESCRIPTION

DESCRIPTION OF EVENING.

WRITTEN IN THE COUNTRY.

THE eve's in dufky mantle dreft,
The day's laft gleam juft ftreaks the Weft;
Till flowly finking from the hills,
A deep'ning fhade the profpect fills.

No found to ftrike the ear doth move,
From rural pipe or vocal grove;
The flocks and herds to reft are gone,
The hamlet's wonted fports are done.

The gathering clouds now clofe arrange,
As waiting for the coming change;
Till Luna and her train in fight,
The fober evening yields to night.